RETURN TO THE SADDLE

James W. Cole

authorHOUSE™
1663 LIBERTY DRIVE, SUITE 200
BLOOMINGTON, INDIANA 47403
(800) 839-8640
WWW.AUTHORHOUSE.COM

This book is a work of fiction. People, places, events, and situations are the product of the author's imagination. Any resemblance to actual persons, living or dead, or historical events, is purely coincidental.

© 2005 James W. Cole. All Rights Reserved.

No part of this book may be reproduced, stored in a retrieval system, or transmitted by any means without the written permission of the author.

First published by AuthorHouse 12/08/05

ISBN: 1-4208-6022-4 (sc)

*Printed in the United States of America
Bloomington, Indiana*

This book is printed on acid-free paper.

Chapter One

The day started out about like usual. I had sent out one wagon loaded with supplies, for the trip over the Donner Pass into Virginia City. That was our best run, from Sacramento, to Virginia City, Nevada.

I was glad to be sending my best hand, Ron Bates, because he could take care of himself. We hadn't had much trouble, but I still felt better about sending Ron on the trip.

Two months ago, Mr. Ronald Bates was up on the pass, near the top, when he ran into some owlhoots. Bates had made camp for the night in a well covered place off the road. To the back of his camp there were rocks, several trees to the front, and a grassy spot off to one side where he had picketed his mules for the night. Bates was aware of the riders even before he saw them. He had stepped back away from the firelight and was standing in the shadows when they rode into his camp.

James W. Cole

Now Bates could be friendly, and would be most of the time, but he was a little short tempered and would be ready to fight at the drop of a hat. "Howdy stranger," Bates said with caution, "step down and have some coffee."

"Don't mind if I do," the older of the two said. Bates noticed that the throngs were off both their six-guns as they stepped up to the fire. He moved in a little closer himself, but just stood watching as they took in all of his camp in a quick glance.

"Been a long day," the older man said.

"Yeah it has," Bates answered without offering any direct information.

"Where you headed to?" the older man asked.

Bates was alone and he already knew what he might be facing, so he was careful not to give them too much edge. "We have a run that comes this way," Bates replied, avoiding his question.

"Traveling alone?" the older man asked.

"Ah yeah," Bates was irritated already and noticed that the younger man was now standing off to one side. Bates dumped the coffee out of his cup and pitched it toward his saddlebags and started out of camp. "Better check my mules," he said as he slipped out. "Help yourself to the coffee."

The conversation had been short, but ole Bates figured to take the fight right to them if that was what they wanted.

A shiver went down the back of his neck as he realized he had turned his back to them, but

Return to the Saddle

his pace had already quickened and he just kept walking out toward the mules.

Out with the mules in the shadows, Bates breathed a sigh of relief. He had gotten away with turning his back this time. Now when he was all fired up, he had the tendency to throw caution to the wind. However, he wasn't real sure of these fellows motives, and thinking on this matter, he tried to figure it out while rubbing on his mules.

Now as he told me later, these cowpokes looked just like cowpokes. Sometimes though, a cowboy will punch cows a while, then ride the outlaw trail a little while, trying a little of both as they go.

Both of these fellows were dressed like cowpunchers--jeans, shirt, vest, hat, and six-gun. Their horses even looked right, with winchester, rope, saddlebag, and blanket. Had he cut them off short? Had he imagined bad intentions? He stood there a short while with the mules, thinking and looking the situation over.

Then he saw something that gave him a little more to go on. The older man whispered something to the younger and the younger turned and walked back toward their horses. Bates wasn't very far from the fire, yet standing behind the mules, in the shadows, where he was out of sight. Still he saw the young man pull his gun slightly, then ease it back in his holster. A reaction a lot of gunmen do to make sure the gun is not stuck in the holster.

The only reason a man does that, Bates thought, is because he is ready to use it.

James W. Cole

Being mostly out of sight, Bates slipped around behind the rocks behind his camp, crossed over to the other side, circled around through the trees, and ended up in front of his camp. He eased up until there was only one tree between him and the front of the camp.

As he quietly observed the two men, he saw that the younger had eased around to where their horses were between him and the mules I had sent him out with.

Did he need anymore? The older man was standing, cup in left hand, standing where Bates should have been looking across the fire at him when he came back from the mules.

Well Bates had to do something, he had been gone long enough now that they would know something was amiss. As he stood waiting, trying to plan what to do, the younger man shucked his Winchester out of the saddle holster. This was it.

"You fellows up to something?" Bates asked. He had stepped a little to the left and behind the tree, just enough for a good field of fire at both of the men.

The young man swung and fired, hitting the tree as Bates had hoped. Bates whipped his colt out and plugged him right in the chest and ducked down behind the tree.

He jumped out on the other side in a crouched position just as two shots from the older man's pistol hit the tree. Bates fired twice at the man standing in the light of the fire. His clear field of fire put both bullets to the chest ending the fight very abruptly. As Ron Bates and I were talking later, he said "That was a bad deal, there is no way to win, even when you are the one left standing."

"Yes, that's true," I said, "My Pa once told me that it's never all right to kill a man, even when you have to. You know Ron, it's a shame those men might have been good citizens with a little help."

Thinking back on all of that, as I watched the wagon pull out. If it had to be only one of my teamsters out there by himself, I was glad it was Ron Bates. Old Ron had fought everything from Indians to owlhoots for a long time. He came west just before the Civil War and had seen a lot.

Bates wasn't none too handsome, thin faced and about forty, slightly balding, although you might not know it. He almost always kept a felt western hat on. At just over six feet and thin as a rail, I suppose those men had thought they could just run over old Ron. Many a man had misread him, he was a real warhoss. If I had to send anyone out alone, Bates was the man.

❖ ❖ ❖

"Good morning, Richard," I said as my shipping foreman rode up with a team of mules and a loaded wagon. "I see you have us another load."

"Yeah, I loaded early on the docks at River Freight, they came by late yesterday and said it would be ready early."

"That's what I thought might be happening," I said, "with a wagon and a team of mules gone." We usually kept most all the wagons at my place out in the edge of the country. There was twelve acres of land on my place, and a fair amount of grass, enough to help feed the mules. When they were not being used, we kept them on the grass.

"Richard, do we have any more loads?" I asked.

"Yeah, Mr. Ford has a load to unload after lunch downtown at the Sacramento Supply House. Came off the docks also, we went down early together. He should be here pretty soon."

"Sacramento Supply, that's where Ben Harrell is. Believe I'll go with Mr. Ford, might get a chance to visit with Ben."

"Well, I'll be here at the office," Richard said, "go ahead and if I need any help I'll get Mr. Ford's grandson, Charles, to help me."

"O.K.," I said. It had been a couple of days since I had seen Ben, not long really, but Ben was a good friend and I enjoyed visiting with him.

Ben Harrell was about fifty or so, fifteen years my senior, a good man, about six foot, thin and fair looking, mustache and gray around the edges, thin faced, but a smart and reasonable man. He was the senior repair man at the supply house and a good one. He could repair most anything-- lamps, stoves, household, or working material.

I was looking forward to our visit when as Richard hitched the mules he said, "we need to

Return to the Saddle

swap out these mules, carry these to the grass and bring some more in."

"All right," I said, "I'll carry them in this afternoon when I start home."

"John," Rich said, "That's good, but I'll come over early and catch up two teams. We have to send this load out in the morning. It's going to Jim Wester's over on the Comstock."

Jim Wester was our agent in Virginia City. He was an excellent businessman, good friend, and our agent for freight. With so many different ways to ship nowadays it wasn't easy with wagons, but if there was a load to get, Jim could get it.

"Just one wagon, Richard?" I asked.

"Yeah, you know how it is, good to get that sometimes, you know."

"Well, who's in line to go out next, Fuller?"

"Johnson is next, Fuller is off a couple of days." Richard replied.

"That's good," I said as I thought back to the events of two months ago. Richard was a good foreman, ran the business most of the time. At about five-feet, ten inches, Richard was a hair shorter than me. He had sandy blonde hair, slightly balding, and was a little hefty, but so was I. Rich was a good friend, neighbor, and good help. A good member of the church, as was Ben and myself. I liked Richard being around, whatever was going on.

We went a long way back, Richard and I. We went to school together, hauled freight back East and came West together. That's how we met Jim

James W. Cole

Wester. We had stopped over in Virginia City for a couple of years, worked around, met Jim. I was able to make a deal with him then. Only thing was, we had to come on to Sacramento.

Noon came, we had dinner at the office and Mr. Ford, an older man of about sixty, and I went over to the Sacramento Supply House to deliver this short load. It didn't take long to find Ben. He was in the back repairing some outdoor lamps as I walked in. "Howdy neighbor," I said.

"Hey man, " he greeted me with a handshake and a smile. "How's it been goin'?" he asked.

"Aw, pretty good, I guess, the wife is about to get used to the place out in the country, and business is holding on. How about you?" I asked.

"Well, this place has so many investors, you can't always tell. But I'm doing all right. Say, I was about to catch up, what do you say we ride over and see Pastor Guest, see how the repair work is going on the church."

"I'm riding with Mr. Ford, I really should help unload," I replied.

"There's plenty of help here," said Ben, " and I'll drop you off at your office later."

As we arrived at the church, we immediately saw something was wrong. There was too many people there just for repair work.

"John, Ben!," the pastor exclaimed, "you're just the two we need. The Green's little five year old girl, Bessie, is missing."

Chapter Two

"Bessie is missing!" Ben said rather excitedly.

"Yes, this morning, at their home on Elm Street, she was out playing in the yard when Mrs. Green noticed she wasn't there anymore," the Reverend explained with a grim look on his face.

"I looked everywhere!" exclaimed Mrs. Green as we huddled together in front of the church.

"I reported it to the Marshall, my husband George is out looking, I just don't know what else to do," she said with a sad look on her pretty face. The Green's family was about like mine--husband George, 35, wife Emily, 28, the children were almost reversed, Robert, 9, and Bessie, 5 years old.

I was thinking of my own kids as they were talking. My daughter, Marie, nine years old, and my son, Benny, just five months. My wife, Melissa, would be just as excited as everyone else here. These people were good people, but I didn't know why they wanted us.

"What did the Marshall say?" I asked.

"He said that he would do his best, but he didn't know for sure," Mrs. Green explained.

"Why us, Pastor?" Ben asked.

"Why, that should be obvious, Ben," the pastor explained, "all those years in the army that you had, and John, an experienced Indian fighter, frontiersman, and with contacts from here to Comstock. And everywhere else in this part of the country too. And Ben, I know that you and John really care, and that you will do your best. God speed, Gentlemen, and my prayers go with you."

Well, we climbed into Ben's carriage, not knowing what to think. It seemed as if we were pulled into something that was not our doing.

"Ben, it seems that one wiser than us, King Solomon, said 'withhold not good to whom it is due.' These are good people, Ben, and that's an innocent child that is missing. We should do our best."

"I agree completely," Ben said, "let's get to it."

"Drop me off at my place," I said, "we'll touch base in the morning, make as many contacts as we can today."

As Ben rode off, I already had several things in mind. It was mid-afternoon, and I immediately began to look for Richard. I found him out back of the office at the small shed where the mules stayed while at the office in town.

"Richard, you about finished here?"

"Yeah, got the mules ready to go out to the farm."

Return to the Saddle

I explained the problem to Rich about Bessie as best I could and told him that we had been asked to help. "Richard, Ben's with us on this, he is checking with the Supply House customers. Why don't you check out the docks, ask Sam at River Freight, and the others. I'm going down town. Tell Charles to watch the office."

Mr. Ford's grandson Charles would be at home. School was out and he worked for us part time. They lived only three houses down the street.

Two of the places downtown were easy enough to check out, customers of ours, but the third place gave me a kind of uneasy feeling. I could not skip it though, information could be picked up there.

First, I went down to the saddle shop, Beldon had customers from all over. He and I swapped trade quite often. When we finished talking, Beldon agreed to do some checking and get back to me. The same thing happened at a couple of other places. Everyone was willing to help, but nobody seemed to know much.

It was getting late, after five p.m., I knew that I could put it off no longer. I stepped down off the buckskin I sometimes rode, felt of the .32 caliber derringer I kept in my vest pocket and stepped up to the door of the saloon. It was a saloon of the sorts, but most of the business men stayed away. They went to more classier joints across town. Me, I just went home, my family meant a lot to me. I suppose that is one reason I was so ready to search for little Bessie.

I stepped through the swinging doors of the Cantina, as they called it, and eased up to the bar. "Afternoon," I said as the bartender faced me. A husky looking man with a beard and an apron.

"What'll you have?" he asked.

"Just a sodie water and a little conversation if you don't mind, Barkeep," I said.

"Suit yourself," he said.

I looked around as he went away for my drink. I knew what he was thinking, why come in for no more than that.

There were a few people sitting around, not as many as there would be later. About halfway down the bar stood a man in a Stevedore get-up. He was sipping on a beer, not seeming to notice me or anyone else. He was a little taller than I was, but about the same weight.

"There you go," the bartender said.

"Thanks, I was wondering, if you had heard anything about a missing girl?" I asked.

"Depends," he said, hesitating, "is she grown, married, or what?"

"Just a little girl," I answered, "five years old, gone right out of their yard this morning."

The man at the end of the bar kind of half straightened and hesitated with his drink. Did that mean anything? Did he know something?

"She was playing in the yard and her mother noticed she was gone," I continued, "they looked everywhere."

"Well--," the bartender started.

Return to the Saddle

"Why don't you go where you belong city slicker?" the man down the bar intruded.

"I thought this bar was open to everyone," I said.

"Please, no trouble here," interrupted the bar keep.

"You and that fancy suit of clothes, you don't belong here. This is a bar of the hands that ride the trail," he said. He didn't really look like a cowhand, more like a freighter or a dock hand.

I turned back to the bartender, trying to avoid confrontation of any sort. "Mr. Barkeep, have you seen or heard anything?"

" I told you to get out of here!" the man down the bar shouted as he started toward me.

He came at me and swung a left at me. I stepped back and ducked down at the same time, a trick that wouldn't always work. I guess I looked easy to him. As I came up I shoved him out toward the tables. He stumbled and fell, turning over a table and spilling its contents.

I knew I would have to be ready this time, he would be more careful. He jumped up and ran to me. I stepped aside and he ran into the bar, but he was ready this time. He immediately turned and swung that left at me.

This time I fell down and backwards, a move I knew would put me on the floor, but hopefully without his blow. To salvage the move, I kicked out with my right foot. It caught him in the chest and speeded my fall to the floor.

James W. Cole

I landed face first on the floor, not knowing if I was about to get my ribs kicked in or what. I bounced up like a cat, not because I was so fast, but because if you were slow, you might die.

I looked around, and saw that my blow had sent him sailing across the room. I stepped over, and just as he was about to raise up from one knee, I kicked him in the forehead with my instep. He just flipped over backward, hit the floor, grunted and rolled over.

"You had better get going before the Marshall gets here," the bartender said.

"Thanks," and I turned to go, checking for my derringer, grabbing my hat and paying for my drink.

As I arrived home with the mules, my wife met me outside the front door. "John, is something wrong, you're late?"

"Richard didn't come by?" I asked.

"No, I haven't seen him."

"Well, there is a problem," and I explained about Bessie and the days events.

"Oh, no!" she exclaimed, "what are you going to do?"

"Just pray and keep looking."

My daughter had been listening closely. She looked up and said, "Pa, please find her, she's my friend."

I had a beautiful family, a pretty wife and daughter, and a son beginning to grow and do things. I looked at my family and realized the Green family was not happy or complete tonight.

Return to the Saddle

The next morning I was up just after daylight to the smell of coffee, eggs, and bacon. I had come to enjoy the comforts of home as opposed to the three years we spent moving from Mississippi to California. We would move a little and stop, one year in Texas, one year in Colorado, and two months in Virginia City.

We had tried several things and it didn't work. Then the two years on the Comstock, we knocked about at mining. Melissa worked as a waitress in a café and I worked in a mine. Richard and I worked together all the way across.

"Honey, breakfast is ready," Melissa called from the kitchen. She didn't always cook breakfast, sometimes I did.

"O.K., be right there," I answered. "Have you seen Richard?"

"Yes, I saw him out the window. He had caught some mules and was leaving the others in the barn."

"I meant to be ready and ride with him. Slept late I guess."

"Honey, be careful, please, I don't want you hurt."

"I'll do my best," I said. "Breakfast was great." I finished as quick as I could, and then saddled the Appaloosa. Banjo, I called him, his movements were like music.

As I rode in to the office, I saw that the loaded wagon was gone from behind the fence.

"Good morning, Richard," I spoke as I met him out front.

James W. Cole

"Have you seen Ben this morning?" I asked.

"No, I haven't. Met Bole Johnson early, and got him going."

"Did you tell him about Bessie?" I asked.

"Hot Dawg! I shore didn't. He was ready when I got here, so we hitched up the mules and he took off."

"Well, it might not matter anyway." It was only a few minutes until Ben arrived, we compared notes and discussed the problem. Ben asked, "Do you think that guy at the bar knew anything?"

"I don't know. He could have, or perhaps he just wanted to pick a fight. I do think I'll ease back over there and talk to that barkeep again.

We split up after that and went our separate ways. We tried to cover all of town as best we could. So far nothing had turned up. I had the cold feeling we were losing the trail. Not that we had anything to start on, we still didn't.

The bartender was wiping glasses when I walked in later that morning. The place was empty. The bartender was most eager to talk when I laid some money on the table.

"I had wanted to tell you yesterday," he said, "about an outfit specializing in underhanded projects. Don't know too much about them or where they are at, but you hear things sometimes about them moving stuff. You know--guns, merchandise, even people."

"Do you think that guy that started the fight was one of them?" I asked.

"Could be," he said.

Return to the Saddle

I eased on out, climbed up on that Appaloosa hoping that I could see Ben, Richard, or the Marshall.

Within two hours I had seen all three. However, this was just enough information to get started on. We went home that night the same way.

The next day was the same. Nothing. Then, late that afternoon after closing time, Ben and I were sitting and drinking coffee when Richard came busting in. "Sam, down and River Freight, just told me about that bunch. He found out from some of the Stevedores that six or seven men left out yesterday with a wagon and several horses."

"There was a man and a woman with a small girl that looked like Bessie. However, the thing that was odd was a camp outside of town and the riders were all armed."

"Could that be her?" Ben asked.

"We have got to move on it," I said, "sounds too close to let it slip by."

"Also, we don't have anything else right now and we can check out that campsite before dark," Richard said with excitement in his voice.

"We can check the camp for a sign of Bessie," Ben said as he grabbed his hat.

Chapter Three

Richard led us to the camp as it was described to him. It was about a mile and a half outside of town to the Northeast. This was a surprise to us, we were half expecting Bessie to be carried aboard a ship and down river.

I had sent telegrams to our agents of freight in San Francisco, Stockton, and other points to the North and East in hopes of heading off any flight. There was also the possibility that Bessie was still in town. Just to cover all points, I had telegrammed Jim Wester in Virginia City.

"We can't overlook the possibility that this is a wild goose chase!" Ben exclaimed.

"That is true," I agreed.

"I think we are on to something," Richard replied, "Let's give it a chance."

We rode up to what appeared to be their campsite about an hour before sundown. We stepped down out of our saddles and began to look around. I began to read the signs on the ground, that will quite often tell much of the story of what they did and who they were.

Richard looked for a minute and wandered off in the bushes. Ben walked off in the direction that they left in. I could see by the signs of about seven men and after some looking I saw a woman's footprint. Only one, but it was enough. Nothing of Bessie.

Ben came into the campsite first. "One wagon, possibly a coach, and six or seven horses headed East. They could go toward Placerville or over the pass from here, I'm not sure."

"Anything to indicate Bessie being in this bunch?" I asked. I was beginning to think what Ben had already said, a wild goose chase.

"No, the wheel tracks, and the horse-shoe tracks indicate rich people, traveling close, but no girl."

At that moment, Richard came tearing out of the bushes at a dead run. There was a little cover around, and the campsite was well picked. "Hey, fellas," Richard called as he came running, "look a here," he ran up to us. "This is the doll I saw Bessie with at church Sunday. There was also tracks of a woman and a little girl."

We were looking at the doll when a bullet spat dust beside us. Nobody had to be told to hunt cover. We had all been shot at many times, and hit on a few occasions. We ended up in the bushes in three different places.

I saw that everyone was moving and heard no other shots, so I kept quiet. I looked in the direction that the shot would have come from and was sure the others were doing the same. I had my .45 Colt and Richard had grabbed his revolver as we left the office, but Ben didn't have his gun, since the trip was sudden and short.

Suddenly, Richard fired and I saw dust fly from a rock 100 yards away in the direction we had been looking. My Colt would be no better than Rich's now. A good Winchester was needed, but the horses were out of reach.

Two more shots rang out as our enemy tried to pin us down. Richard fired again in return. I knew Richard would be still, return their fire, and wait for me to move. We had done this many times before, and it had worked well for us.

Off to the side was fair cover and I took off hoping not to be seen. About halfway I stopped to look around to be sure this was right. Looking back, I could see where I had left Richard and Ben. They had better cover than I thought. Ahead there was some small rocks, and some more brush.

Suddenly something moved behind me. I dropped to the ground flat on my back and swung my pistol over toward the noise that I had heard. Ready to fire, I was suddenly glad that I had learned to be sure of my target. There stood Ben Harrell with a .45 Colt pointed directly at me.

With relief we both lowered our guns.

"Let's go," Ben said, and took off toward the rifle. I had to move fast to keep up with this man, fifteen years my senior, a friend now about four years.

Return to the Saddle

In no time at all we were behind the man with the rifle. A couple of shots had been fired, but we were ready. Ben stepped out a little and then to his side.

"Drop the rifle," Ben commanded, "slow and easy."

"You're covered twice, hand," I said.

Suddenly aware that we were there and had the drop on him, he slowly eased the rifle to one side and dropped it.

"Care to do some explaining?" Ben asked.

I waved my hat in the air four times side to side. The standard signal to Richard.

"Look ah, ah, ah, take it easy," the man said with a shaky voice, "I didn't hurt nobody."

"Just what are you doing?" Ben asked.

"Gimme a chance?" the man asked. Sweat popped out from his forehead.

"I thought you guys were outlaws."

"Come on man, we don't care to play," Ben said, and cocked his .45 for the first time. "Talk."

"O.K., ok, a man about your age, only heavier, paid me $100 to watch the campsite a couple of days and if anyone found anything to scare 'em off."

"Who was he?" Ben asked.

"I don't know, he just paid me and took off."

"Let the Marshall deal with him, Ben," I said.

Richard came up with our horses, and we rode by and left the man with the Marshall.

❖ ❖ ❖

James W. Cole

Early the next morning we were far out on the trail, starting before daylight we were at the campsite at dawn to pick up the trail.

Just before I left home, I asked the Good Lord to keep my family safe and keep my steps as I tried to help put back together another family. Later, I had learned that Ben and Richard prayed the same prayer.

We picked up the trail, and sometime later we followed it into the Donner Pass Trail. We then picked up our pace because Richard and I knew most of the turnoffs and could check them quickly. We had crossed this trail many times with wagons.

We had made good time most of the way. The first day we saw several people, but none had seen our hunted party. The second day we didn't see any sign or people to speak of, but kept going. The third day we saw what could be sign of our party, but too much time and too many riders had passed over. We also passed Bole Johnson on the way.

It was almost dusk on our third day when we saw a lone wagon up ahead. He was moving, but we would catch him shortly. He never looked back to see who we were, just kept riding.

We rode up beside him and he said, "John, are you lost? What are you doing up here?"

"Ron, recognized you right off, how are you making it?" I asked, glad to be up with him.

"Everything's fine, be there on time, mules'r fine, coffee's good. Y'all out for a joy ride?"

"Let's set up camp and I'll tell you all about it."

We found a good place, set up camp, and began to settle in with coffee, beans, and beef jerky. Ron was a real card, and was enjoyable to be around. "Must be some big to-do, ole John got that spotted horse out. I thought you didn't do anything but pet that ole mule."

"Ah, Ron, you know Banjo is a good horse," I said. Ben and Richard were grinning, listening to Ron clown around.

"And just look a there, got that big gun out. I thought you had lost that thing," Ron said, and looked over at Ben and Richard, "He may fire that big gun off here, if we don't watch, get all excited and just fire that thing off."

"Now, Ron," I said, "You know this is a .45, like a lot of men carry."

"Well, compared to that pop gun you carry in your pocket, that .45 is a big gun," Ron retaliated.

"Yeah, I guess so," I replied. "Ron, seen anything unusual the last couple of days?"

"Not too much, you know what's out here, usual bunch, headed to or from the Comstock."

Up until now Ben and Richard had sit back and enjoyed the fun, now they jumped in the conversation as Ben said, "Seven men, a coach, a woman, a small girl."

"Yeah, and heavily armed, running close, and cautious," added Richard.

"Yeah," said Ron, "Yesterday, just after dark. I was camped off the trail kind of out of sight and they passed by. I don't think they saw me. I didn't count 'em but probably seven riders. There was a coach, nice looking, one driver, that's all I could see. It was unusual that such a party was moving after dark."

"Ron, the little girl is from our church. She was taken from near her home, stolen from her parents and carried away, and we are trying to get her back," explained Richard.

"They left probably twenty-four to forty-eight hours ahead of us," Ben explained, "and it looks like we have gained very little on them."

"They could be swapping horses," I guessed.

"That, and traveling through most of the night," Ron suggested.

"We can't afford to ride at night, we might lose their trail," Ben said, "although we don't have much of a trail, we can watch the turnoffs."

"What do you plan to do?" Ron asked.

"Well, we have to catch them first," I answered.

"We have to do our best," Richard said, "we can't let this thing go. I wouldn't want my daughter lost."

"I agree," said Ben, "we must establish a plan, stick with it, and somehow get that little girl back for the Green's, for all their sakes."

Return to the Saddle

All was quiet for a little while. No one said much, for we thought of that little girl. She was lost somewhere, possibly all alone, certainly with no one she knew, not knowing what would happen next.

"Ron?" I asked, "How did you know it was us, this afternoon, coming up behind you on the trail?"

"Why, John," Ron retorted, "you know the answer to that. A man must watch his back trail if he expects to live. I saw that Appaloosa way back and knew it was you. I figured the others were Richard and Mr. Ford, although it is nice to see Ben, I figured you were out on freight business."

"Ben?" I asked, "that reminds me, the other day at the camp, I understand a good army man slipping up behind me, but where did you get that .45 from, I had it figured that you were unarmed."

"That was a good one, wasn't it?" Ben grinned as he answered, "it was a holster sewn in sideways, under the back of my coat. I got it when we first started this deal."

We laughed and cut up a while before we turned in. I always enjoyed these times best, besides those with my family. I sure hoped everything was fine at home. Mr. Ford would check on them, be sure they were all right, but still it wasn't like being home.

The Sierra's were always so beautiful. The higher up in the mountains you climbed, the tall-

James W. Cole

er the pine trees grew. Ponderosa pines they called them, and lakes and streams almost everywhere.

Tomorrow we would cross the Truckee River several times. It was always cool, clear, and pretty. I always enjoyed taking it slow and easy around this river, but we had something more important at hand.

❖ ❖ ❖

At dawn, I was walking out a ways from camp. Viewing the beautiful sunrise. God graces us with his beauty often, and we do not realize it. Today, I realized it. "Lord," I prayed, "I desire to do your will, to serve you, help us find this little girl and return her home. Lord, I ask that there will be no shooting, I don't desire to kill anyone or even hurt them, but this little girl must be returned home. Thank you, Lord, for wisdom in this matter. In Jesus name, Amen."

Breakfast was ready, we ate and saddled without much talk and rode on out. We expected to be in Virginia City the next afternoon unless the trail led otherwise. Ron Bates would be an extra day arriving and we couldn't wait for him.

It was late when we arrived the next day in Virginia City. Jim Wester would be gone from his office. I thought he may have stopped by the saloon on the way home, so I stopped. Ben and Richard went on to the hotel.

I stepped into the saloon and looked around, Jim Wester wasn't anywhere to be found. I stepped

Return to the Saddle

up to the bar and ordered a sodie water. One or two cowboys laughed, others didn't seem to care. "Seen Jim Wester?" I asked the bartender.

"No," he answered, "if he comes, it's about time, but he doesn't always come. Sometimes he goes to the new café down the street."

"Thanks, I'll wait," I replied.

"Hey man, you in the wrong place ain't ya?"

I looked around to find a rough looking miner sitting at a table behind me. "Not unless I was hunting the preacher."

That caught him off guard and he just turned away. I decided to make good use of the time and ask the bartender about Bessie. "Barkeep, you heard or seen of a party of six or seven men, a coach, and a woman and a small girl about five years old passin' through?" I asked when he stopped nearby.

"What kind of coach?" he asked.

"I'm not sure, rich folks maybe, well armed, the man's about fifty, slightly gray, about 185 pounds."

"Well, I'm not sure," he answered. He was about to say something else but the man next to me at the bar interrupted.

"Tenderfoots ought to be at the General Store eating licorice. Think I'll just make you eat dust instead."

Chapter Four

I immediately looked at the bartender and asked, "Does he say that to everybody?"

"No," he answered.

"Does he say that to you?" I asked the man on my right and took a step backward.

"No," he said, "can't say that he does."

I turned to the miner that had spoken earlier, "Has he fed you some dust?" I asked.

"No, of course not," he retorted.

I stepped past the man that was waiting to make me eat dust on my left. "Does he say that to you?" I asked the next man at the bar.

"No," he answered. By now quite an uproar was taking place. This did what I had hoped, the bad hombre took his eyes off me and began looking at everyone else.

I just eased around a table and out the door. I saw what looked like the new café down the street and kept walking. I didn't want to hang around to give the guy another chance.

Return to the Saddle

Jim was seated in a corner toward the back. He smiled and stood up as I approached him. We shook hands and he said, "Sit down friend, it's been a long time, how have things been?"

"Just great, Jim," I answered, "everything's fine, I am well. Had a good trip over and saw the old trail again."

"I got your telegram," Jim said, "I have asked a few questions, but not answers yet."

"Jim, I wished circumstances could be different, we--" I stopped short. The bad hombre from the saloon just walked in the front door. "Jim, know that guy that just walked in?"

Jim didn't have time to answer.

"Get up and slap leather or die where you sit," the hombre shouted from the door.

I knew Jim always carried a gun, even though I didn't see it. He didn't put up with any nonsense. However, I didn't really want to drag him into this, it wasn't his fight.

I still had my .45 strapped on from the trail. I still didn't want to use it but now there was someone else to be concerned with. If I could slip out the side door, Jim would be left to face him alone. I wasn't scared of him, the point was, why should I kill him?

"Are you in a hurry to get killed?" I asked.

"You're not getting out of it this time," he said, moving to his left. He now stood in front of the window causing me to have to look at him with the outside behind him.

James W. Cole

"Mister," I said, "sometimes you avoid a fight, sometimes you face it square on. You want to fight, this time you've got it."

I stood up and moved away from Jim. I didn't want my friend catching a stray bullet.

"Why is it that you pursue this thing?" I asked.

I didn't get an answer, he went for his gun, an emptiness hit my stomach, possibly a little fear. However, I didn't hesitate. I whipped my .45 out so fast it even surprised me. His gun was clearing the holster and in an instant I saw there was no time to play. I fired and a second later his shot whizzed by my left ear. I had taken one step to the right, a safety precaution I'd learned from an old gunfighter some years back.

My bullet had smashed him in the chest and carried him backward, as most large caliber guns will do. He hit the plate glass window and fell through to the sidewalk outside, his feet hanging on the window sill.

Jim jumped up and ran to the window. I walked over to join him. "Lord help!" I exclaimed.

Jim peered out the window and said, "There's no help for him."

"I was meaning me," I said reluctantly.

"He called it," Jim answered, "and yes, I do know him by the way. He's a hired gun. I don't know what his last venture was, he has been gone from here for several weeks."

I stood and looked and thought, then suddenly it came to me. "Jim, this man challenged me in a

Return to the Saddle

bar in Sacramento before we left," I said somewhat disturbed. "Yeah," I continued, "he had on a Stevedore's outfit, but now I remember he didn't sound like one."

By now quite a stir had been created. As I stood looking, Jim paid for his meal and the plate glass window, proving just how much of a friend he really was. We stepped outside and met the Sheriff. Jim explained what happened and the Sheriff turned us loose.

We had just started to walk away when Rich and Ben came running up. "What happened?" Rich asked excitedly.

"The guy from the Cantina in Sacramento didn't like me asking questions here any more than there," I answered pointedly. "Oh, by the way," I said, "Jim, you know Rich, meet Ben Harrell, Ben this is Jim Wester." They shook hands and greeted each other.

The rest of the evening passed without event. We stayed in the hotel that night, walked all over town the next day digging for information and found nothing.

Late that afternoon Ron Bates made it into town with the freight wagon. I was glad to see Ron, although I didn't know what he could do. At least he was here and safe.

I explained to Ron about the shooting. "Ron, that man was a gunfighter and connected to the bunch that took Bessie. Go by the undertaker and take a look, see if you know him and look around, see if you can find out anything."

"O.K. Bossman," Ron answered. Ron was tired, but he would do his best.

❖ ❖ ❖

Next morning early, Ben, Rich, and myself had breakfast with Jim Wester. We were discussing the problem at the new café when Ron Bates came in. "Good morning, John," he said.

"Sit down, have some coffee," I answered.

"Thanks," Ron said. "The hotel clerk told me where you were; Hello, Joan," Ron looked up at the waitress, "just leave the pot. I was up half the night."

She smiled rather pertly at Ron and set a cup of coffee in front of him and went back toward the kitchen.

"You know that gal?" Rich asked.

"Yeah," Ron said, "been coming to see her here and at the old place ever since I started the wagon. Her name is Joan Blakely, good woman."

"Jim, did you know about this?" I asked.

"Well, you don't repeat everything," he said.

"John, the reason I was up half the night was 'cause I was running down some leads on your gunfighter. His name is Rudy Birdsong, or it was. Hired gun, worked for a number of shady characters including one over by the capital."

"Know who it was?" I asked.

"I am not sure," he said, "Bar Q, or something like that, thought I'd ride over and check it out, unless Jim has a load for me."

Return to the Saddle

"Nothing that won't wait," Jim said.

"Take off Ron," I said, "Ben and Rich and me will check some of the nearby ranches."

Ron gulped down his coffee, gave the waitress, Joan, a light peck on the cheek and out the door he went. Outside he mounted one of Jim's horses, he usually borrowed when in town and took off.

Ben got up to leave, "If you fellows will excuse me, I am going to ride to the east and look around."

"I'll go North," Rich said as he finished his coffee.

"Jim, if you will ask around town, I'll follow Ron as far as Silver City and look around," I added as I also finished breakfast.

"You got it," he said.

Too late to catch Ron, I simply saddled Banjo and eased on out toward Silver City, which was almost half way to the capital, Carson City.

Seeing Ron and Joan sparking together reminded me of my wife before we married. We used to ride together on Saturdays and Sundays. I had a big black horse *(that was all I had)*, sometimes we rode double, sometimes we picked up a horse.

I remembered her pretty face, shining eyes, and beautiful smile as she looked at me. It seemed that all was well with the world when we were together. We both were much quieter then, and being together was more than enough whether we talked or not.

I remember holding her little hand, looking into those gentle eyes, and seeing the warmth and love that she had for me.

When we were married that smile was still there. She made trips with me in wagons in Mississippi hauling freight. She would sometimes drive a second wagon with me on the trips.

She still hated to see me go off without her. Sometimes the tears would well up in her eyes and we would stand for long periods of time just saying good-bye.

Thinking about it I remembered that she sometimes would slip a note in my bags that I would later find down the road. I looked in the left saddlebag, the one place I had not looked since I left home.

There it was. While riding slowly down the road, I read the note. "Please be careful and come home soon. I miss you, Love, Melissa." Oh how I wanted to turn around and go home. Those eyes, those smiles, Melissa, Marie--my daughter, and Benny--my young son, it was worth all the trouble of home and work.

Banjo jerked his head up and I realized we had slowed to a crawl. I clucked to him and we quickened our pace.

Meanwhile, Ben's ride wasn't so pleasant. Following the Truckee River east, Ben noticed someone on his back trail not long after he left the Comstock. Ben had angled North and East to pick up the Truckee River and he had noticed someone on his back trail for some time.

He came to a place where he had to cross the river to go on and that's when it happened.

Chapter Five

Just as Ben was in the water crossing over, a shot rang out. The Big Black held steady. Ben enjoyed the finer things in life and horses were no exception. That big black was a fine horse.

Ben immediately dove into the water. He did that to both protect himself and the horse. He scrambled for cover. Looking, he saw that the shooter must be up high. Along the river here there were mountain ledges and cover all around. It was the reason he had to cross the river to start with.

The black horse took off for cover, being well trained. Ben had found a big rock near the waters edge for cover. He had the patience of an Apache Indian. He had fought his share of them, and he sat real quiet for over an hour. There was no better cover than what he had. He didn't have his Winchester. The Big Black was out of sight, and his clothes were even beginning to dry.

The pass here where the river ran through was about three hundred yards wide. Ben could

Return to the Saddle

see from one side to the other. Nothing was happening. Ben wasn't about to, for a minute, presume the shooter was gone. That's how you got killed.

The Black whinnied in the distance. Ben took it to mean something had disturbed him. Pulling his black felt hat down he ran across to a small clump of bushes, tall enough for cover. He took one quick look and ran again to the side of the mountain and behind a large rock.

There he settled in to watch back toward the rock by the river where he had first taken cover. The sound of the Black had paid off. In just a couple of minutes, a man appeared off to the side. There was cover, but it was scattered.

Ben started out behind the gunman and suddenly a shot dug into the rock behind him. Ben turned and fired twice up on the side of the mountain and dove back behind the rock where he had been.

His plan had been great for one man, but there was two, maybe more. Suddenly Ben realized how much trouble he was in. Our plan had been, seek information, locate the enemy, but not to confront.

Ben had a real confrontation on hand. He popped up and fired twice at the man in front of him. Return fire was given immediately from both men. Suddenly he saw a crack in the side mountain behind him. Upon closer examination he saw it led further down the side and not through. This

James W. Cole

would put him under the shooter on the ledge and away from the one on the flat.

Ben slipped down the side of the mountain and past where he thought the man was above him. As he did so, he wisely replaced the four spent shells in his six-gun.

Ben had considered himself a loner for years. He had been through many situations by himself. He had not been blessed with a lot of friends as some people. He and his wife Deanne had been content for years to keep to themselves. He had called me the first real friend he ever had. So, facing this problem alone was nothing new.

What was happening? Had the first shooter come down off the mountain, or was the second man on the flat the whole time? Ben shuddered to think he could have been shot when he first moved.

He didn't panic though, that was very dangerous. He had walked a short distance when he heard a rock tumble. He looked behind him and the man he had seen on the flat emerged from behind a rock. Ben squeezed off a shot that took the hat clean off the man's head.

The man swung wildly around and fired at Ben hitting the side of the mountain well above Ben's head. Ben fired twice more, hitting the stranger in the chest and knocking him back against the rocks into the dust.

Thinking the other man would come down to where his buddy was, Ben took off the other way. He was about to turn a corner when a rifle barrel

Return to the Saddle

slipped out from behind the side of the mountain right in front of him. Ben quickly holstered his six-gun and grabbed the rifle and jerked it.

Instead of the man coming with the rifle, he let go and ran the other way. Ben checked the rifle quickly, peered around the corner, and fired twice at the running man. Ben wasn't a back shooter but the varmint had tried to kill him. He quickly saw the rifle was way off and threw it down, drew his gun out and gave chase.

Ben gave chase at top speed past clumps of bushes and then quickly pulled up a turn on the side of the mountain. This was a small hole in the wall and either the man was waiting, gun in hand, or had run past the hole.

Studying the ground around the crevice, Ben began to see some sign. Suddenly Ben dove inside the hole and behind a rock and began to look back out in the open. Just as he did two shots hit the rock above him. He fired the three remaining shots left in his pistol at the stranger and ducked back to reload.

The man had not ducked into the hole as one might think, but instead ran past it and circled to get a vantage point as Ben had jumped behind the rock. He was no dummy. He wasn't a bad shot either. Now Ben was bottled up.

The strangers rifle probably had been dropped or the horse had bumped a tree or rock slightly bending the barrel, not enough to see, but enough to cause the shots to miss. He wouldn't miss the next time.

James W. Cole

Ben looked around and saw there was nowhere to go. It was about forty feet to the back of the hole. There was one more rock and a little brush, but very little to help.

To wait until dark could be a help to Ben, but it could also help his adversary. Ben might could slip out under the cover of darkness, which wouldn't be long in coming, but the man could get closer under the darkness.

Suddenly Ben whistled. Then he whistled again. This unnerved the stranger and he began looking to see what would happen.

The Big Black came racing out of the bushes and straight toward the stranger. The stranger, being unnerved, ran out in front of the horse. The Black just kept coming, as now the shooter was between Ben and the horse.

Ben saw his chance and made a break to the left to get out of the hole and in a better position. The stranger couldn't stop the horse any other way so he shot him point blank. The Black turned and ran off. By now Ben was following the path the stranger had taken.

Ben ran around a clump of bushes, a couple of rocks and was behind the stranger. That is if he was still where he had been.

No sound could be heard as Ben stopped to catch his breath and listen. The horse was gone, the shooter was quiet. No way to know for sure where he was.

The man he was supposed to kill was not dead, the horse he thought he shot in the chest, just up

Return to the Saddle

and ran off. He had thought he was a good shot, but had missed every time today.

Suddenly he was aware that something was behind him. Before the stranger could move, Ben said, "you call it, hand, you have been trying to call it all afternoon, so make it good or make it bad."

The shooter turned and fired, but he missed again. Ben fired and hit him in the shoulder, not wanting to kill him. The stranger fired and missed again. Ben shot him in the chest, knocking him down into the bottom of the ditch where he lay lifeless.

Ben quickly reloaded his pistol, not knowing what might happen, as this was the west. The western frontier being a cautious place at best, you always kept your gun loaded and if you used it, you quickly reloaded it.

Ben slipped down to check the dead man as he slipped the six-gun back into the right handed holster. He wore his gun on the right, as I did, swung not too low and tied down when needed as it was now.

About this time Ben heard some horses. He dropped down in the ditch near the dead man and peered out to see what was happening.

They found the horses of the dead men and Ben heard one of them say, "look around and see if you can find Ross and Charlie, somethin' is goin' on."

Now Ben knew if these were friends of the bad guys, he was in trouble. It appeared there was four or five of them and that was not good. The spot was not good where he was. It was time to go. They were too close to wait.

Taking a chance, he whistled for the Big Black. Immediately the other gunner dropped from sight. "Where are you? Ross, Charlie?" someone called.

Ben knew that no good would come from any answer, so he kept quiet. They didn't know exactly where he was, but it wouldn't take long to flush him out. Just then he saw one of the men move.

Six-gun in hand Ben knew it was time to fight or leave. As he was considering what to do, suddenly he noticed the Black just behind him among some small oak trees.

Ben ran down the lower side of the ditch out into the trees toward the Black. The Black quivered, sensing his master's hurry. The Black took off as soon as Ben's left foot hit the stirrup.

Ben wheeled him to the side and they headed west toward the river and Reno at a dead run. The Black was big and strong, the rare larger Arabian breed of horse. The ground began to pass underneath in a hurry and Ben pulled his hat down in front a little tighter, as the wind was whipping by very hard.

The other men ran out from their cover and up to the ditch. Just one glimpse of their partner and they started shooting. By this time Ben was out of range.

Ben slowed a little to cross the Truckee River and came out on the other side gathering speed.

Chapter Six

The trip for me was fairly pleasant and short. Silver City was a town not too unlike Virginia City, a town some hoped would be a mining town.

After looking and asking all over town, I turned up nothing. Ron had ridden on to Carson City. I didn't catch him, but he should be all right.

Supper at the hotel had been fair and a few more questions had turned up nothing. I didn't care for most saloons, but again, the place for information was usually the saloon.

"Barkeep, you have any coffee around?" I asked as I stepped up to the bar.

"Yeah, I reckon, some in the back," he said, "some I keep for myself." In a minute he returned, smoke rolling off the top of the cup. "There you go," he said and turned and walked away.

I stood at the bar and sipped on the coffee. It was black and strong, but it was good.

Looking around I was trying to find someone to ask about the little girl and thinking, this was a shot in the dark. Had we lost the trail? Would we

James W. Cole

ever find that little girl? Was Bessie gone forever? We couldn't give up now. This was much too important, we must exhaust every effort.

I sipped on the coffee and looked at the bartender. He was busy and the dozen or so others were preoccupied with drinking, gambling, talking or what not.

Just as I was about to give up, a U.S. Marshall walked through the bat-wing doors. He lightly spoke to one or two and walked up to the bar beside me.

"It is good coffee," I suggested, "looks like I'll be up a while, so I'm drinking coffee."

"Me too," he said, "got to ride to Virginia City, see Jim Wester."

Now I just sipped on my coffee and thought on that for a minute. The barkeep brought more coffee, so I had an excuse to hang around a little longer. Jim was well known and liked and respected, so I decided to take a chance. Sometimes saying you know a man or he is your friend can get you in trouble, especially with the Law.

"Jim Wester's a good man," I said, "I suppose he gets a good many callers.

"I wouldn't be on no social call at night," he said, "some tall lanky, hombre came riding into town, Carson City, and shot a fellow. Marshall Jackson locked him up. He said it was self defense, but the man's gun was still in his holster and it hadn't been fired. He asked for Jim Wester and I was sent. Doubt if he even knows him, but for Jim's sake we'll see."

Return to the Saddle

"Did you see the brand on his horse?" I asked, knowing most western men usually do. I did when Ron left Virginia City.

"Yeah," he said, "J.W. over C, why?"

"Jim Wester Companies," I replied.

"Well, I'll say," he said, "I should ah known that."

"Let me introduce myself," I said, "John Colter, Frontier Freight, Sacramento. We do a lot of work for our friend, Jim Wester."

He slowly extended his hand to shake, "Marshall Henry Durbin, one of the five U.S. Marshals working out of Carson City."

I could tell by the expression on his face that he didn't know what to think of me. "I'll see to your message, if you like, and you won't have to go on to Virginia City," I said.

The puzzle was still on his face as he said, "I'll go on, Jim has been a good friend and help many a time. I wouldn't want to sell 'em short."

He finished his coffee and said, "Good day," and he slipped out and rode off. I finished my coffee and paid the man, then I eased out myself.

It was getting late as Banjo and I eased out of town. There were a few stars shining through, but not many. Marshall Durbin would reach the Comstock before I reached Carson City. I was sure he would ask Jim about me, so I was not concerned about Jim following me right away.

The Marshall also knew the trail, and I didn't. It would be my first time in Carson City.

James W. Cole

As I rode along at a slow pace, letting the Appaloosa pick his way along, I considered what was ahead and what Ron might have gotten into.

Suddenly the Appaloosa jerked his head up and his ears pricked up. I eased on the reins and he stopped. After sitting there a moment I didn't hear a thing. I couldn't see much and could hear even less.

Rather than sit out in the middle of the road and prove a good target I eased down off the road and turned Banjo around to face the road.

It was might quiet, no crickets, no birds, nothing was making any sound. What was it? The App's ears were still up. I looked and listened. Nothing. Was it a cougar, a wild Indian, an outlaw, was there more than one?

Suddenly I wished I was off the horse and down on the ground. Down where I could hunt for some good cover. To dismount now would make the saddle leather creak and possibly cause Banjo to stamp a foot. Just be still, I thought.

Suddenly off to my right I thought I saw the vague outline of a man. My first impulse was to draw, but by now he had the advantage. Chill bumps ran up the back of my neck and under my hair. Fear comes upon all of us sometimes. I remembered the Good Book says 'fear not', so I waited for it to pass, and it did.

"Looking for something neighbor?" a man with a cool low voice asked. He couldn't have been more than twenty to twenty-five feet away. How did he get that close? A lot of hunters and trackers

Return to the Saddle

could move quietly and leave a little trail, but this beat all I had ever seen.

"I was on my way to Carson City to see a friend," I replied.

"You're a little off the road, and not moving very fast," he said with a deliberate and even tone.

I thought as he spoke, western men don't often give their names. You don't know if it will be good or bad for them to know who you are. I decided to take the chance.

"My name is John Colter. I'm from Sacramento. Some other men and myself came over to Virginia City looking for this little girl." He was quiet as I explained, "It has been unusual. You don't know what will happen next, "I concluded.

"I was in town when it happened," he said, "heard a little about it. If you will go to the Trails End Saloon, ask an hombre named Robert Cooly about it, you might learn something. Watch his left hand, if he holds it out a little and starts rubbing his thumb and fingertips together, he's about to draw. It's a distraction, mean joker."

"Thanks friend," I said, "I'll do it."

"By the way," he said, "Names Sheridan, foreman of the Rocking R Ranch, which you are crossing a small part of right now. Stop and have coffee sometime."

"Well, thank you sir," I said, "I will."

I clucked to Banjo and he eased out up in the road. I looked back to glimpse the man I was talking to. He was gone, nowhere to be seen.

It was getting even later when I rode into Carson City, the slow ride, the talk with Sheridan, took just about three hours from Silver City. Most of the town was quiet as I rode down the main drag.

Up ahead a place was still open. As I rode up to it, I saw the sign overhead. Trails End. So this was it. I dismounted and stepped up to the bat-winged doors. I slipped the throng off of my six-gun. This could be the one Sheridan told me about. I stopped outside.

It got quiet quickly. Four or five cowboys were lounging around, some drinking. Looked like maybe they were about to close. I easily swung wide to the right, away from the bar.

"Robert Cooly?" I said with enough volume that everyone there easily heard me.

"Who wants to know?" a man at the bar said and then turned on a stool to face me. He had a possum grin on his face and looked like he was ready for trouble.

"I was told you might could tell me about the shooting that happened here today. A tall rider and a local guy shot it out."

He was still grinning as he said, "Now who would say that?"

"Sheridan," I said.

The grin slowly faded and he stepped to his feet, as if anticipating trouble.

"He seemed to think something happened other than what was said," I guessed.

Return to the Saddle

"What's it to ya," he sneered, "you stickin' yore nose in where it don't belong stranger?"

"The man in jail is my friend and it's a lot my business, besides he never pulls a gun unless he's forced to," I said pushing him.

"Mister, I expect you had better leave," he said. He was standing straight up, looking straight at me, rubbing his fingertips against his thumb.

"Go for that gun and it'll be your last," I said pointedly.

His right hand jumped for his six-shooter. He had already started his move before I drew and fired. My bullet hit him in the chest as his gun fired.

I went down to one knee and swung my gun to the right and fired taking a man's hat off that was sitting across the room.

At that moment the saloon doors swung open and a rifle leveled off straight at me and fired. I swung my pistol around at the door and then back to the man whose hat I shot off.

"Ho Mister, I don't want no part of this," he said with a scared look on his face.

"Hands on the table," I said to him.

He eased his hands on the table very slowly. I glanced to the back of the room. There was a dead man in the back, laying across a table. Cooly was also dead.

I looked toward the door. "Joan, you're a long way from the Gold Miner's Café."

"I rode out not ten minutes after Marshall Durbin came in the café. I have ridden the trail

James W. Cole

from Virginia City to Carson City a number of times. I know it well."

"I'm glad," I said with relief, "somehow, I missed that man in the back."

"I'm glad you look before you shoot," she said.

"Well, I was taught to know my target," I answered, "That's why I only shot this man's hat off. I didn't see a gun." I reached down and picked the man's hat up and laid it on the table in front of him. "My apologies sir," I threw a ten dollar gold piece beside it, "buy a new hat."

"Thanks," he said.

The Marshall busted through the door about that time and said, "Alright, everybody hold it."

I had already holstered my gun and Joan lowered the muzzle of the Winchester to the floor.

"What happened here?" he asked waving his long barreled six-gun around the room.

"Are you Marshall Jackson?" I asked.

"Yes, I am, but I want to know what's going on here," he said with a low stern voice. He was about fifty-five years old, grey around the edges, but obviously battle-wise, and tough as whetleather.

"Well sir," I said, "I was asking these gents about the man you locked up today and they didn't like what I was saying. He just drew on me."

"That right Frank?" the Marshall asked the man sitting at the table. He still had his hands on the table and the hat, and ten dollar gold piece was where I had put it. Sweat had popped out on his forehead.

Return to the Saddle

"Yeah," he said just loud enough to hear.

"What about this afternoon?" I asked, "did you see that?"

"Yeah," he said, same tone of voice, "Cooly talked ole Red into calling out the stranger, and when the stranger beat Red, Cooly slipped Red's gun back in his holster when no one was looking, so's you would think it was murder, said he'd kill me if I said anything. I was scared to leave even, afraid he would think I was going to rat on him."

"Truth is stranger," the Marshall said, "we have had trouble out of Cooly for some time."

"Marshall," Joan spoke for the first time since the Marshall came in. She was pretty, dark haired, dark eyed, and likely a good woman for any man. At about age thirty, she was still young and well able to hold her own, as was the case with the rifle and the man in back.

"Marshall," she said again, "when I stepped in the door these two had John in a crossfire. I threw down on the one in the back to keep him off John."

"Ok," the Marshall said, "I've heard enough, let's go get Bates out of jail."

A smile came across Joan's face quickly and brightly and it was easy to see why she came.

"If you came for Ron, how did you end up here?" I asked partly joking.

"I saw that Appaloosa and knew you would have something in mind," she said.

The Marshall released Ron and we rented some rooms at the hotel to finish the night out. It was puzzling to think that three men were dead and we didn't know why, or did we? Ron had been asking questions about Bessie and just as before someone had interrupted before an answer could be given. Coincidence, I was beginning to wonder.

Chapter Seven

We were in the saddle early and arrived back at Virginia City by noon as the pace was much faster. We found Rich, Ben, and Jim at the Gold Miner's Café. Joan stowed her rifle and went right to work, jeans and all.

"You fellers get lost?" Rich asked. As he was quick to talk a lot of the time.

"Yeah, rode around in circles all night," Ron said with a grin. He was as quick to joke as anyone.

Joan was there almost immediately with coffee, "I'll bring you beans, taters, chicken shortly, if that's ok"

Everyone nodded approval and I began to explain what happened. As I described the details no one had any good answers. Ben told of his trouble up on the river, and that seemed to add to the confusion.

"One thing is for sure, we are not hunting gold. We're looking for a little girl and we can't give up," Ben said with a solemn look on his face.

James W. Cole

"Ben," I said, "You go to Carson this time and I'll ride up the river towards Ten Gallon where you were. Rich, you and Ron carry supplies for a couple of days and go back to where we last saw their trail, check it out, work back this way."

"I have some more people around to talk to, " Jim said.

❖ ❖ ❖

The afternoon wore on as me and the App rode North and East toward the Truckee River. With fresh supplies, I was prepared to stay out a couple of days myself. Whatever Ben ran into might be waiting on me. If it was, I would have to face it, our leads had been few since arriving on the Comstock.

The Appaloosa was a good horse. He had rested some at Carson, so had I, but we didn't have a lot of time to waste.

The crossing where Ben had trouble was just ahead. If it was connected to Bessie and somehow they knew who we were, they might be watching for me. Now, come to think of it, they might know who we were. We had asked everywhere we stopped, the story was spreading rapidly, a lot of people were beginning to know about Bessie--and us.

I made the crossing where Ben was at before and rode on. No problems. I tried to put the pieces together, but I couldn't.

Return to the Saddle

I began to pick up tracks as I rode through the area. I saw where Ben was at and scattered parts of where his battle had taken place, but there was nobody about, alive or dead.

The tracks agreed completely with Ben's story, as an experienced tracker can read into a story by reading the trail. I could see how the battle had taken place.

I began to ride off to the East. I could see tracks of seven or eight horses. These fellows had probably loaded up their friends body's and headed back home or where they came from.

Now, my idea was to follow and see where they came from. I wanted to know. If this was a bunch of outlaws, I would just avoid them and ride off. If it was something to do with Bessie, I needed to know.

The country was pretty. I followed their trail, which followed the river. There was a small range of mountains on my right, maybe two hundred yards off and a higher range of mountains off to the left about the same distance. It was flat down in the bottom--some grass, a few trees that weren't very big, some bushes, but not many.

It was a pretty place. A body could raise horses, cows, or both here without too much trouble. The pass narrowed going in, ran about the same for four or five miles and then began to widen out again. The river followed a natural course right through the bottom. There was no want for water here. The river was still strong, cool, clear, and pretty.

James W. Cole

I was guessing that, straight through, it was about twenty-five or thirty miles West to the Sierras, by way of the river. We did not come through Reno. We had turned South toward Virginia City. The trail was more used down at the bottom and we had lost the coach. We also wanted both a good supper, and rest for ourselves and our horses and to see our friend, Jim Wester.

I was following their trail, watching as it seemed they were riding at a normal gait, when they edged up closer to the river like maybe they were going to cross. I slowed and eased along side of the bank. I was looking at the tracks, then over in the river. It was about a twelve or fifteen foot drop to the water here, and not a good place to cross. Why so close to the edge?

Then I noticed a blade of grass in the toe of my boot. Where did that come from? I don't remember getting down off the horse. My wife Melissa says that I'm too picky, don't like dirt on my hands, stain on my clothes, or dust or grass on my boots. I bent over to pull the blade from my boot toe.

Suddenly a rifle shot rang out and I heard the whizz of the bullet as it went over me. Now, when someone is shooting at you, you don't worry too much about where you are going to land, you just jump. I kicked loose from the stirrups and dove into the river. I didn't even raise up, I dove the way I was leaning--into the river.

Return to the Saddle

Only thing was I landed in shallow water. Now there are rocks in this river all the way from the top down--and I landed on one of them.

Boy Howdy, it knocked the daylights out of me. I lay there a second trying to catch my breath, my head just barely above water. I couldn't get enough air to come in to do me much good. I had to move, they would catch me out in the open.

I rolled over and almost went under. Struggling, I managed to get to my feet. The water was cold and the current fairly strong. Not too strong for a healthy man, but I was staggering. I took a couple of steps toward the bank. Maybe I could take cover under the bank.

Just as I was getting close to the bank, I saw a hole under a tree root. If I could just get in there, I thought. I took a step toward it and staggered again. I grabbed the tree root and pulled, and hoped there wasn't anything there.

I fell into the back of the hole and lay still. Nothing in here but mud and a little water, and I can't stand dirt on my hands. No matter.

Then, I heard a racket up above. "Where's he at?" one said.

"I don't know," the other one answered.

"Where's his horse?"

"I don't know."

"Well, they couldn't have just disappeared," he said, their voices getting louder and louder.

Come to think of it they would have had to be shouting for me to hear them above the tumble of the water. I still wasn't breathing enough. What did I do? Suddenly all went black.

Chapter Eight

I awoke with a start. Water was in my ears. I sat up rather quickly. The hole was filling with water. It was dark as Egypt. I scrambled for the hole which should have been in front of me.

After feeling around I discovered the open hole was under water. I must have climbed three or four feet after entering the hole.

I couldn't stay here, this hole might fill up with water. My air supply was already limited to what was left in the hole. It would be much harder to get out later.

Like it or not here we go. I reached down, grabbed the open hole, pulled myself under and out. Immediately the current grabbed me and jerked me downstream.

Swimming was not one of my better talents, but I surfaced shortly. I was close to the bank but going downstream rather hurriedly. Lightning flashed overhead revealing a huge rock just in front of me in the now pitch black darkness.

Rain was falling and must have been for some time. How long had I been out? I grabbed for the rock but slipped off the side and kept going. It only served to remind me how sore my chest was.

Lightning flashed again as the rain fell and I saw a tree limb hanging down. I reached out in darkness to where I thought it was and grabbed it. The limb bent but it held and I began to pull myself in.

Sitting on the bank, soaking wet, no hat, no slicker, I began to check myself. No cuts or breaks that I could tell. My chest was sore, but other than that I seemed to be okay.

I felt for my six-gun. The throng was still in place over the hammer so it was still there. I felt for the derringer, it was still there, for the vest pocket was a tight one. Both guns would have to be cleaned for there had been a lot of mud, although most washed off on the ride downstream.

I slowly stood up and began to walk back upstream. It seemed to me the snipers were downstream or somewhere to the East as Ben and I both had encountered them while traveling East.

I walked for some distance, maybe four or five-hundred yards. I couldn't tell. The rain was still falling. I had to find a place to get out of this weather, build a fire, and dry out. The snipers might be out there, but not likely. They would be curled up somewhere in a warm place and it wasn't likely they'd move.

Return to the Saddle

Lightning flashed again and the horse's nose bumped me in my sore chest. Then I was sure it was Banjo. He had come back to find me. He nickered and I said aloud, "Thank God, somebody's praying for me."

I breathed a sigh of relief and said, "Boy, it sure is good to see you."

I climbed aboard and swung North hoping to find a ledge or overhang in the edge of the mountains, some shelter from the storm.

I checked for my saddle gun. It was there, a seven-shot Winchester, an early model but it was still in good shape. It was mounted on the right side, stock at rear, barrel at front. I had chosen that way for just this kind of situation. With a small hole on the lower side of the barrel end of the boot, what little water went in the stock end of the boot would drain out the barrel end. At least I would have one gun that would fire.

The occasional flashes of lightning helped me to keep a good angle toward the mountains. My pa once said 'there are different kinds of storms, sometimes the lightning comes straight down to the ground, sometimes the lightning goes side to side and never reaches the ground'.

Tonight the lightning was side to side, I was glad. I felt a little better about riding in the storm. I also remembered my pa saying 'Lightning goes to the front of the storm. The clouds and the rain always follow the lightning'.

That was another comforting thought. The lightning seemed to be moving away.

There was a nice overhang in the first two hundred yards of mountain range. I moved in underneath the twelve to fourteen feet high ledge and stepped out of the saddle.

I found some dry matches in my saddlebags and some scattered wood about and built a fire.

Soon the coffee was hot and camp was in order. I didn't know how late it was, my railroad pocket watch had stopped when the water hit it. No matter how late, the thought of cleaning my guns, rubbing down my horse, and drying my clothes was necessary.

The morning broke fair and pretty. When I awoke the sun was already beginning to rise. Upset at myself for sleeping past daylight, I skipped breakfast and saddled right away.

The App seemed better rested than I did. My chest was still sore, however, there was no restriction in movement. I didn't think there was anything broken. Why I passed out I still wasn't sure.

I mounted and began to ride back to the West. I could go to Reno or back South to Virginia City. I had ridden only a short ways when the thought hit me. What was it Pastor Guest had said, 'an old Indian fighter'? I had survived the night 'Thank God', I wasn't going to quit.

I swung Banjo back toward the river going East. I was going to Injun' around and find out who this bunch was. I was not going to let this thing beat me. Now was not the time to forget what I had learned, but to remember well.

Return to the Saddle

I crossed the river as soon as possible. It had gone down some and was not difficult to cross. This time instead of looking for a single trail, I was looking for men.

There wouldn't be any trail to follow after the rain, so I would look for camp, hideouts, or line shacks. I stuck low to the ground, staying off of hilltops where I could easily be seen.

The first thing I found was a line shack, backed up against the mountain as it began to break away to the East and open country.

From a concealed place I sat and watched for about three hours. The shack looked like it had been used so I was determined to hang in there. Whoever would come could tell me if there were any gangs operating around.

There were a few trees around, not many, mostly oak and not too big. Otherwise it was the mountain behind the shack and open country to the East and North back to the river.

After a few more minutes passed, a couple of riders came up to the shack. They dismounted and went in. My thought was to find out who they were or what they knew. It wasn't that far back to where I was shot at.

I patted Banjo on the neck and said, "Stay." I was up wind and not too far from the cabin. I figured about twenty minutes on foot and I could be up side of the cabin listening to them.

It took that long too, to slip up on them and not disturb them or the horses. I almost arrived too late. "The boss said find him, and like it or not we might as wells ride on," one said.

"That horse is a dead give away," the first one said. "That App's white splash can be seen a mile off," he added.

"Yeah, and we found his hat, just look for a rider on an Appaloosa with no hat," the second one said, "no need hanging around here, let's go."

They mounted and rode off West where I had been. "There's about fourteen men looking, we'll find him," I heard as they rode off.

As they rode off I slipped in the shack to look around. There was nothing specific in what they said, so I looked to see if there was any hints inside.

None at all.

As I plundered around I discovered a hat and a jacket and suddenly I had an idea. It might not be easy to slip by fourteen men going East along the river. I remembered when we came West from Denver we used the lower route to Virginia City.

It was about fifteen miles, or maybe twenty, South of here, but if I made good time I would be close to it and well away from these fellows by nightfall.

I checked to make sure the coast was clear and took off for my horse. The hat and jacket were a close enough fit, so all that was left was Banjo.

I grabbed the reins and lead him until I found what I wanted. I grabbed a handful of mud and started rubbing it right behind the saddle.

Return to the Saddle

I had learned that trick back in Mississippi as a boy during the war. I had a white collie dog that chased rabbits and squirrels, sometimes through the mud. It would darken his hair and stay for awhile, sometimes until it was washed.

With all of this completed, I mounted up and headed South. I stuck to the low ground as much as I could to avoid everyone. About two miles or so I reigned up. Off to my left, about three hundred yards, was two more riders headed, possibly, toward the line shack where I was at.

They couldn't have seen me for more than a minute. What now?

Chapter Nine

Suddenly I threw my hand up and waved right to left twice. One of the two riders did the same and I turned to ride on.

I rode a short distance to make it look good and turned to look back. They were nowhere in sight. Hopefully to them I looked like one of their hands, with the hat and jacket, riding a black horse.

I urged the App into a nice canter, one he could hold the rest of the day, and we started eating up the countryside.

At dusk I realized I hadn't eaten anything all day. I found a secluded spot and made camp with coffee, beans, and some biscuits left from Gold Miner's Cafe--dry and in fair shape in the saddlebags.

At dawn I was in the saddle and about an hour later I picked up the trail for Virginia City and headed West.

I stopped only for water and ate beef jerky while riding. How many times had I done that?

Return to the Saddle

It was dark already when I arrived at Virginia City. I left my horse at the livery stable, paid the man to wash Banjo, and walked down to the Gold Miner's Café. It was late enough that most folks had eaten and gone.

There was not any of my bunch here, just Fred. I walked in and took a seat in the back, with my back to the wall. I had heard that Wild Bill always sat with his back to the wall. I had picked up habits here and there and there was too much going on to take chances.

I looked up and Howard was grinning. Howard Downs was a black man, and also a friend of mine. Howard would pray with you or grab a gun and ride with you, just whatever. Howard was a good man.

He brought me some coffee, since there was no one else around at the moment. He was still grinning. Then I remembered the black, flat crowned, flat brimmed hat. I sheepishly pulled it off and laid it in the chair side of me. By now Howard's grin had progressed to a chuckle.

I looked up and smiled back and said, "It's a long story."

He poured the coffee and said, "Want some supper?"

"Yeah, I'm starving, almost anything will do."

"Steak and taters?" he asked.

"Yeah, that's fine," I said. "Have you seen any of my bunch?" I knew that he knew them, we had eaten here a number of times since being in town. Howard was the cook and a good one too.

"Jim and the fellow with the mustache, ah-Ben, was here for supper."

I nodded an approval as he walked away. So Ben had beaten me back, huh? Well, the distance was shorter anyway.

Wonder what he found out, if anything? I sipped on my coffee and tried to figure it out. Shootings in Carson City and shootings over close to Ten Gallon. Miles apart, but not that far apart.

You heard of Gunfights from time to time, but you didn't see them everyday. It was those Easterners that thought every town had a gunfight at noontime everyday.

Why we had men and women to die of old age out here, even if no one else thought so.

So there must be some connection and there was a chance that they knew who they were shooting at. I sure hoped Ben could tell me something.

Howard served me up some steak and potatoes that was great. I ate every bite and cleaned my plate. Then I thought of my family back home, Melissa's suppers were usually her best meals. And suddenly I wanted to be at home.

Not at all the image of a tough guy, but then I wasn't trying to be a tough guy. I sipped my coffee and thought about Melissa's long brown hair and beautiful smile, and the kids. Marie, with her pretty smile, like her mother; and Benny, his little giggle when you tickled him. It was such a joy to have a beautiful family.

"Howard, do you have paper and pencil? I would like to write a letter."

"Sure," he answered, "coming right up."

We had been gone about two weeks and it was past time to write home. As I sipped my coffee, I began my letter:

Dearest Melissa,

I miss you honey. We have been in Virginia City several days now. Some trouble, and we still haven't found Bessie yet. We are not giving up though. We expect to hang in there until we find her.

Honey, I miss the long walks, the horseback riding, the long talks, and the happy times together. I realize a man's place is at home with his family, and I desire to be at home with you and the kids. There is no greater joy than to see the smile on your face and to hear the laughter of the children.

Honey, if I were chasing the gold, it would not be worth losing my family. The fame would not be worth it. Bessie is a real live human being, a child, a part of someone's family. That's the only reason I am still here.

I love you Melissa. I love you Marie. I love you Benny. I always will. There may be problems in life, but by God's Grace we will make it.

Love always,
John

James W. Cole

I look back and remember how hard it was for me to say those words at one time. Now I was more mature, a changed man, with a different outlook on life.

I finished my coffee, paid for my meal, and headed down the street to the Sagebrush Hotel. The clerk there would mail my letter. It was late so I turned in, hoping a new day would bring us closer to finding Bessie.

Early morning found us all at the Gold Miner's Café discussing the problem at hand. The coffee was hot and the eggs and bacon were good. Ben was telling of his trip to Carson.

"Marshall Jackson didn't know any more than what he had told already. He seemed to think it was just troublemakers. Nothing else turned up either," Ben said. Rich and Ron had ridden to the foot of the Sierra's and back and arrived in about midnight. That part of the country, north of Virginia City, we knew real well.

"We didn't turn up a thing boss man," Rich said, "not even a jack rabbit."

"Nothing here either," Jim said.

"Fellas, think about this," I said, "I was shot at, nearly drowned, hunted by at least a dozen men and just barely made it out over close to where Ben was the other day."

I related the events as well as I could about everything that happened including my return trip.

"Could be just outlaws," Jim said, "they like to cut that main trail sometimes, they make a pretty good haul, then pull out before the law can catch up."

"If they don't have Bessie, I just simply don't care to waste time fooling with them," I said.

"Yeah, and if she's not there we would be wasting time," Ben said sternly.

"What do we know for sure?" I asked.

"Wealthy people," Ron said, "that coach was first class and seven well equipped riders, it takes more to have that kind of escort."

"We know they came down off the Sierra's on this side," Ben said. He was the oldest among us and the best tracker. "They could have gone north of the river instead of south like we did," he added.

"We have been in four gun battles, here at Carson, and two over by Ten Gallon," I said, "the only one we know for sure that is connected to Bessie is the one right here in this café," I added.

Joan was pouring more coffee. Ron was looking goggle-eyed up at her and as she started to pour his, he jerked his finger away from his cup and shook his hand about three times, blew a little bit like the hot coffee burnt him.

Joan hit him lightly on the shoulder after she finished pouring his coffee and grinned and said, "Oh, stop it, I didn't burn you."

He looked around at us and began to laugh. Joan just turned and went on about her work. Ron was always up to something like that. He had rather have a big joke going than anything.

"You better be nice to her," Jim said, "you won't find another like her."

I got up to pay my bill, "Fellas, nose around here, sleep, rest, let the horses rest, whatever. Let's just hang loose today and see what happens.

They nodded and mumbled their approval and I slipped out the door.

Pastor Jerry Robbins was an old friend in town that I hadn't seen yet. He was my next stop. I felt I needed some good advice.

Chapter Ten

The church was down at the edge of town. I turned to my left and started down the boardwalk and then stopped. The newly replaced window in the café kind of stood out at me.

I looked around at the building, it was about fifty feet wide in front and about one-hundred feet long, front to rear. It was nice. Business and places like this was a main interest of mine, other than family and church.

I was just looking it over, thinking this was new and it was a good deal for these people. I looked down at the boardwalk, it was new and sturdy, not much chance of falling through.

As I was standing there looking around I noticed a horse and rider walking slowly by on the other side of the dusty street. The rain had long since left the street and it was dry.

Most riders passed by without being noticed, but several people had stopped to watch this man ride by. I looked again. He wore a black hat, had black hair, black shirt, black pants, his boots, horse, saddle and even gun belt were black. With a light tan I began to see, to some, this would be a striking figure.

Suddenly my mind began to race. Had I seen or met this man somewhere? Did I know him or know about him? I looked down at the back of my left hand, my eyes went across my knuckles and out to my fingertips, as though there was an answer there.

Of course! My hand had grown extremely tired from holding the reins still for so long. I looked up and he was gone, nowhere to be seen.

I broke and ran across the street to the livery stable. It was across and down from the café about two hundred feet. I ran all the way across and turned down the alley just as I made the corner of the livery.

Down the alley I ran, fast as I could and stopped at the back of the livery barn. A set of pens about six foot high had been built since I last saw the backside of the barn. Nothing to be seen this way. I looked across the pens and saw the rider at the far corner about three hundred feet off and riding away.

I pulled the loop over my six-gun hammer so it wouldn't fall out and ran toward the first gate. I ran through the first pen without breaking stride.

I ran through four of the pens quickly. There appeared to be about six pens across and if I hurried, I might catch the rider before he rode out of sight. Then I saw a gate that was closed, but I was determined to jump over and keep going.

Return to the Saddle

Suddenly, as I was swinging over the top rail, my heart jumped up in my throat. It was too late now, I was already committed. I hadn't seen him before, I guess the gate had hidden him from me. There was the biggest longhorn bull I had ever seen.

He looked like he was just waiting for an excuse to tear the place down and me with it. My feet hit the ground and I just kept running. The bull snorted and jumped. I didn't want to wait to see what he was going to do.

I made the next two pens much faster than the first four. I looked back and the Longhorn was in the other end of the pen we were in. I looked down the trail and the rider was just out of sight.

Then I noticed someone was behind me just laughing himself silly and I recognized the chuckle. I turned to see Dale Ronson, an old friend and owner of the Washoe Livery Stable.

I had missed the rider so I walked back to the edge of the barn to where Dale had stood. His laugh was so contagious, as usual, I began to laugh with him. His bright teeth shining from under his beard. His six foot two inch heavy frame shook from the laughing. At about two-hundred twenty pounds, I was glad he was a friend. After a minute or so of laughing, I thought maybe he'd settled down enough to talk for a minute.

"What, in Sam Hill, is so funny?" I asked.

"You went one way and that bull went the other," he said between chuckles. "We have been trying to figure out how to get that thang loaded on a

James W. Cole

wagon for two weeks now and hadn't done a thing yet. What we need to do is just turn you loose on him, won't take long that way," he laughed again.

"I don't know about that," I said.

Dale and I had become good friends. It had started at church when I was here and grew from that. He was not always at the livery, so this was the first time I had seen him. His six foot two inch, two hundred twenty pound frame made him bigger and taller than myself. He looked like he could just grab the bull by the horns and throw him in the wagon.

We shook hands and he said, "I heard you were in town, but I didn't expect to see you flying over a fence the first time. What were you doing anyway?"

"Trying to catch the rider on the black horse."

"Do you know who that is?" he asked.

"Well, I have an idea, but you tell me."

"He's the man the tough guys don't mess with. Name's Zane Sheridan. He sure knows how to handle men and himself real well. If you're after him, you better be careful."

"No," I replied, "I would just like to talk to him. Met him briefly the other night, in the dark, out between Silver City and Carson City."

"Yeah, the Rocking R Ranch, that he's foreman of, has a little dog leg that runs through there. If you want to talk to him just never mind his going out of town the back way. Just ride out to about where you saw him and turn south. You'll run into the main ranch house about two hours later."

Return to the Saddle

"I suppose you heard why we are here. Well, Sheridan gave me some good information that night in the dark. Even though I didn't see much of him, we had a good conversation. I have and idea that he can tell me a great deal more," I said looking off into the distance.

"Yeah, I heard," he said, "I'll saddle your horse and you might just catch him."

"Will you be around the next few days?" I asked as I mounted Banjo.

"Yeah," he answered, "I'll be close by."

"I'll look you up if I can," and I clucked to Banjo and rode south of town.

Sometime after dinner I was riding south of the Carson City trail and I had picked up Sheridan's tracks on a trail I was supposed to be going on to their main ranch house. I was eating beef jerky and sipping a little water to keep going.

I knew it was his horse for I had studied his tracks by the livery stable while Dale saddled Banjo. The size of the horse, the shape, and the distance of the tracks let me know it was him. Also, these shoes had recently been put on his horse. The ridges at the back of the shoe and the nail imprints were easily seen.

I had stepped down out of the saddle twice to water my horse and fill my canteen. Sheridan might not could tell me a thing to help, but I had two questions in my mind, the rough crowd over toward Ten Gallon and the things Sheridan had told me about Carson City.

James W. Cole

The Ten Gallon bunch could be just outlaws on the take or a very nervous bunch of cowhands or they could be trying to hide something, like Bessie. Sheridan had sent me right to the source of trouble with Ron, he had told me exactly what to expect. I had begun to think he knew a great deal about things around here.

The trail narrowed somewhat ahead and I slowed, taking precautions as I went. There were tall pines and a few larger rocks on either side of the trail. The Appaloosa pricked his ears and it raced through my mind, what had I gotten myself into now?

Chapter Eleven

Suddenly an antelope jumped and sped away off to my right. I smiled with a little relief, and eased back in the saddle. I reached down to pat Banjo on the neck to settle him down when the crack of a shot whipped across over my head.

I shucked my rifle out of the saddle holster and hit the ground running to my left all in one action. Two more shots rang out as I hunted for cover.

I didn't take time to see where the shots were coming from. I assumed from close to where the antelope jumped. I dove behind a fallen tree and lay still for a moment. No sound.

These guys were laying wait for me. Sheridan's men? I didn't think so. They could have followed me from Virginia City and after they were sure of my direction, they probably circled around ahead of me.

I was in a jam. I had better start thinking, praying, everything I could. There were trees and rocks around, but none close by.

Then I noticed a stick laying close by. I thought for a second, and then I reached and got it. Then, I put that old, flat topped, flat brimmed, borrowed hat on the end of the stick. It was my thought for two things, to be sure they were still there, and to determine how many were there.

I shoved the hat above the edge of the log, and two shots hit the hat almost simultaneously. It flew off away from me and the log about twenty-five feet, and two more hit it again. Sweat popped out on my forehead.

By now they knew I wasn't wearing it. I knew there was two of them and they were ready. I looked at the hat, now about forty feet away, it was torn all to pieces. They didn't miss.

What did Ben say? The first bunch he ran into up on the river were not that good with a gun. If so, and if this was the same bunch, they had sent better gun hands this time.

I looked past my feet to the other end of the log, nothing there. There was no cover close by. The way they hit the hat the second time, they must have a high point advantage on me.

Suddenly there was a rifle shot, then another. It sounded different than the first two. This was a Winchester '73, like mine. The other two had sounded like Henry Repeaters. Not much difference, but enough to change the sound. There were no bullets landing close to me.

I turned and scrambled to the other end of the log. Just then a horse thundered from down the

Return to the Saddle

creek off a knoll and back in the direction which I had came.

I squeezed off a shot from where I laid, and missed. He was moving from my left to my right. I levered in another round and fired again, and missed again.

I lie still for a moment. "Oohh!" I cried aloud. Then suddenly, fed up with it all, I jumped up and ran after the rider. I ran about a hundred feet and stopped behind a tree.

I jacked another shell into the barrel and fired again, but this time he was just too far away. Sometimes lying on the ground is not the best place to be when firing. Looking across the ground or over a hump or uphill or downhill will throw your aim off, and cause you to miss.

Then I remembered the other shooting and the other man. A third party had to have stepped in. I looked back toward the creek and the mound and there he was. "Come on over," he said aloud.

Sheridan displayed such confidence, it was amazing. Again I wished that this man and I had been acquainted before now.

I slipped a few shells back into my Winchester as I walked over. "I told him to drop it, and he turned on me," Sheridan said. This muscular man, about six feet one, was just standing there looking. I knew I wouldn't have to worry about him. His gun would be already reloaded and he would be ready to go shortly.

"I heard the shots and came back," he said.

James W. Cole

"I'm glad you did, " I said, "I was pinned down."

"I knew you would follow me," he said, "I thought it would be safer if we left Virginia City separately. Guess I was wrong."

"They followed me," I said, "see the brand?" I motioned to his horse, tied in the bushes. The Circle G brand was clear on the brown range horse. It was then I knew that the ranch at Ten Gallon had something to do with Bessie.

"That's the same bunch that ambushed my friend Ben Harrell, and then me up on the Truckee River."

"So I heard," Sheridan answered, "ever since our little conversation the other night, I have been stirred up about this. I was a part of a war that was fought to free the slaves."

"Come on, I have something to show you. I'll send one of my men back for this one."

"How did you know I'd follow you out of town?" I asked.

"Well, I guessed at part of it. As for your seeing me, I waited 'til you came out of the café to mount up and ride by. The rest just fell into place. Come on," he said as he mounted that big black horse, "about an hours ride."

I rounded up Banjo and off we went in a westerly direction. It wasn't but about ten minutes until we ran across one of his ranch hands whom he instructed to pick up the dead body and carry into town.

Return to the Saddle

We began to climb in elevation and almost immediately the pines were taller and more plentiful. The ground was rich with grass. There was probably plenty of game, streams of water, a good place to live or to hunt and fish.

We climbed out on a hill and I almost lost my breath. First the small valley was so beautiful. Then I saw the band of Indians. My first thought was that we may be in for a peck of trouble.

"It's hunting party," Sheridan said, almost as if he were reading my thoughts. "Paiute Indians, Red Cloud is their leader. There's nothing to fear, these are peaceable and are our friends. Red Cloud is rumored to be some kin to old Chief Winnemucca. He came along at the last of the big battles."

"It is also rumored that he was a big part of the fight at Pyramid Lake in 1860. The Paiute' won a big victory there, but since then they have lost big."

"Old Chief Winnemuca's daughter, Sarah, has done a lot for the Paiute', even wrote a book a couple of years back."

"Sarah?" I asked, "an Indian name?"

"The Paiute call her Thocmetony. Shell Flower in English."

By this time the Indians had seen us, so we rode down to meet them. Three of them rode out to meet us. They were well armed but I held my peace. They might be peaceable, but probably would fight if provoked.

James W. Cole

There were between twenty and thirty in this band, and they did appear to be a hunting party, but I was still uneasy.

Sheridan made a gesture with his hand and said, "Peace, friend."

The one I presumed to be Red Cloud gestured back and said, "Peace my friend."

"My friend, John Colter, has traveled far seeking a small girl that was taken from her family. He and his friends have worked and fought hard trying to find this little yellow haired girl. Would you tell my friend what you told me?"

Red Cloud looked back to the north and for a moment I thought he wasn't going to speak. Then he said, "For many years my people hunted antelope, deer, rabbits, animals from here to strong waters you call Columbia River. Few of my people see the Columbia, but Red Cloud see Columbia."

"I see day when Paiute was great in war and mighty hunter. I see many things. We fought white man, Ute, Navajo. We were sold for slaves far to the south.

"Now we live on white man's reservations. Where not enough to eat. No Buffalo Robes to warm. We hunt here because Sheridan, good man. He says hunt here for meat and Robes."

"I see Indian take white child. I see white man take Indian child. First time Red Cloud see white man take white child, Red Cloud not understand."

"Maybe not ten days pass, as you call it, at night, we come down from Pyramid Lake to hunt. We make camp late at night. Good camp, no one see. Wagon come, riders come, we see them, they not see us. Wagon break down, horses tired, people tired, woman and child get out wagon. Child run, woman catch, woman say, 'get on horse'. Child say 'you not my mother, I want to go home my mother."

"Red Cloud know child not belong."

"Why didn't you stop them?" I asked.

"Red Cloud belong Reservation. White man see Red Cloud, white soldier come take Red Cloud back Reservation."

"Tell my friend who these people were," Sheridan spoke to Red Cloud.

"Silver-haired man with woman and child, Gunther, big ranch on trail from waters you call Pyramid Lake, to here," he said with great poise.

As we rode away I thought about what a great man Red Cloud was. He would probably never be known as well as old Chief Winnemuca but a great man nonetheless.

Darkness had already fell upon us as we rode toward the main ranch house of the Rocking R. Sheridan's horse suddenly jerked his head up, ears standing straight up, Banjo did the same. We stopped, not knowing what was ahead.

Chapter Twelve

"Come on," Sheridan barely whispered as he eased off the road and in between some large rocks. We turned to face the small trail and sat quietly for two or three minutes.

Then I began to hear something. It was a horse in a slow canter coming up the trail. We sat quietly as he drew near. I began to be a little uneasy about the rider. Sheridan didn't appear to be bothered at all. I hoped my discomfort didn't show.

As the horse and rider rode past us, Sheridan said, "Roger," his voice quick and sharp. the rider turned back and we eased out on the trail behind him. "What's wrong Roger?" Sheridan asked.

"The dead man you sent me to get, was gone."

"Did you find the right place?"

"Yes sir," Roger replied, "I found Mr. Colter's hat, some spent shells, and a blood stain on the ground, but there was not a body."

Return to the Saddle

With that we rode to the main ranch. Supper was late, but good. I went straight to bed. The hour was late and I wanted up early.

❖ ❖ ❖

Early the next morning Sheridan and I were up on the trail that went from Virginia City to Carson City just as dawn was breaking. "If you go straight north you will come out on the rim of a mountain. Follow it till it chops off, then turn east and cross clear water creek. On the other side you will find a game trail that will lead you to Virginia City. Keep off the main trail and a different way back than the way you came. Be safer that way."

"You know that we're going after Bessie, don't you?" I asked.

"Wait until I see Jackson and Durbin. Two U.S. Marshals with us might save some trouble."

That Circle G bunch has given us all a hard time. Wait until daylight in the morning. If you haven't heard from me, then go on."

"O.K." I answered, "daylight in the morning."

He turned west toward Carson City and I headed north across the back trail. His would be a shorter distance to Carson, but he would have the task of explaining a dead body that couldn't be found and talking the Marshals into coming with him.

My task, it seemed, would be to get from here to Virginia City without getting killed, on a trail I didn't know.

James W. Cole

Two hours later I was out on the rim of the mountain and it was beautiful. Ponderosa Pines everywhere. Even though I was on top of a mountain, trees were everywhere and there was plenty of cover. It was no wonder Sheridan liked to come this way when he had business in Virginia City.

I came down off the top as he said and turned east. There was a small game trail to follow most of the way. I stepped down off Banjo and tightened the cinch on the saddle. Clear Water Creek should be close by. I led the App by the reins for about a hundred feet or so, then glimpsed a hoof print.

I knelt down for a closer look. There shouldn't be many riders up here. Then, I suddenly turned cold. It was Sheridan's horse! He was going the same way I was. I was beginning to consider this man a friend. He was supposed to be in Carson City.

Then my mind began to jump. The dead body that couldn't be found, I was on a trail I didn't know, a set of tracks going the wrong way. Was I being set up? I was already kneeling, I turned on the ball of my foot and looked all around. Everything seemed quiet.

I walked on a little further leading Banjo. The trail took a sharp turn to the right and you could see for about three-hundred yards. Then I looked back down the tracks, they were going the other way.

I dropped the reins and walked back a few steps. Then I saw what had happened. Sheridan

Return to the Saddle

had been traveling west, the other way, when he made the turn. He had eased over in the thick grass and rode about a hundred and fifty feet, then he'd turned around and rode back to the sharp turn in the trail. Then, he stopped to watch his back trail a few minutes, then he had turned and rode in the grass again going west. I also noticed by the grass standing up straight that this was yesterday's trail.

Some people said that I was cautious, but Sheridan was years ahead of me. With relief, I mounted up and started riding on.

At the end of the three-hundred yards, the game trail turned back to the left. I could hear the trickle of water from the creek. Then, a big splash!

Then I thought about the tracks, was he really going west? I jumped down, wrapped the reins around the pommel of the saddle and slapped Banjo on the rump. He trotted off toward the creek and I circled the splash.

I stepped out into the open just as Banjo dropped his head for water. Between me and Banjo stood a big man looking at the Appaloosa. I pulled the hammer back on the Colt 45, making the usual clicking noise as it went.

The big man stiffened. Then I knew who it was. "Sorry about that Dale, didn't know who you were." I eased the hammer down and slid the Colt back into the holster. "There's too much going on," I continued, "and I heard the splash of water and felt I had better check it out."

Dale caught his breath and turned. His face was red and it was clear that I had scared him. "Boy you had me going there for a minute. I knew it was your horse, but I didn't know for sure it was you ridin' him. Where did you learn that trick, run the horse one way and you go the other?"

"Ah, I don't know, maybe someone pulled that on me somewhere," I answered. "What was that splash?" I saw his fishing gear. He shouldn't have made such a splash while fishing.

"I was ready to go, I had caught a good mess of fish and an old turtle had sat on that rock yonder the whole time. I decided to see if I could get him to move."

"You throw something big at him?" I asked.

"Yeah, a big limb, by the way, what are you doing coming through down here?" he asked.

"Sheridan told me how to get through here, we had a little run in with some fellows from the Circle G," I answered, "Sheridan thought it would be safer to return a different way."

"Yeah, I heard about that, heard you killed another man," Dale said.

"Not this time. They did spook me enough to let some lead fly. How did you know so quick?"

"Rumors are floating around town. Charlie Bob, my right hand man at the livery, told me at daylight this morning. Sounds like you are between the rock and the hard spot."

"Sheridan's supposed to be reporting to the Marshal at Carson City right now if he didn't get sidetracked," I said as I thought back.

Return to the Saddle

Dale was pulling his string of fish from the river as he said,"He will, he's a real square deal man, count on him when the goin's rough."

"Well I thought so," I said, "did you look around before you left this morning? See any Circle G horses?"

"You know I always look, and yes, there was."

"Can you guess where the rumor came from?"

"You're going to corner a grizzly, messin' with that bunch," Dale said.

"You know that's where the girl is and you know we're going. There's no other choice," I said.

"Boy hydee," Dale said with reluctance, "when you stir up a hornet's nest you really do it right don't you? When are you going?"

"In the morning, early, why?"

"I'd rather be fishin' or huntin', but what can I say, I'm goin' with you."

"Be glad to have you, but you don't have to," I said.

"Yes, I do, you're a friend, and I have children too."

Without much else to say, we mounted and rode to town. My visit to Pastor Jerry Robbins had been on my mind even before I found Dale on the creek, so I left my horse at the livery. After checking on the Circle G horse, that was gone, I walked down to the church.

Dale was carrying the fish to the café. Boy, I sure would like to get back time enough to eat some of that fish. They were always eating fish in the good book. If it was good enough for them,

James W. Cole

it is sure good enough for me. I wanted some whenever I could get it.

I found Pastor Jerry in the back of the church. He was in the study, looking over some papers. He was a friend from the two years we were living in Virginia City. He was thirty-eight years of age, hair slightly thinning up front, about six feet tall, thin, and well spoken.

He looked up when I walked in and said, "John Colter, man-o-man. It's been a long time." He stuck out his hand to shake and I grabbed it. His smile showed his pleasure in seeing me.

"Pastor Jerry, good to see you," I replied.

"Great," he said, "church is stronger than ever, town has settled down some. At least until you came to town," he grinned.

"Well, I'm sorry about that, good neighbor, but it couldn't be helped."

"I know that," he said with the same grin," I was just funning."

"I hate to come see you with a problem, Pastor, but I need to know about some things."

"Well, I'll help you in any way I can," he said.

"You know about why we are here, I guess?"

"Yes, I heard," he answered.

"Well, I have been out of the saddle for a couple of years now. Except for the ride from the house to town and back most everyday. Just a three mile ride. Family, friends, and church has been my interest. My return to the saddle hasn't been what I would have preferred. This deal has been trying."

Return to the Saddle

"I am glad you came by," he said, "I was about to think you had forgotten me."

"Pastor, you know that there have been several people killed. I have tried to be patient, but this is beginning to bother."

"What do you mean?" he asked.

"The teaching in the Bible, 'do good for evil', 'turn the other cheek', 'thou shalt not kill', and I have killed two men now and three others have been killed. Where does it stop, and are we doing this the right way?"

"John, death is all in the Bible, Samson killed many, David killed thousands and he was a man after God's own heart. This is not the first time you have used a gun to defend yourself. You know that the price of freedom comes high sometimes."

"This time the difference is someone else's freedom, not yours, that's causing your doubts. Think about men like George Washington, and Ben Franklin. They were good, Christian men. They had a little money to start with. They gave up a lot for their own freedom, and for the freedom of others."

"Washington knelt in the snow at Valley Forge, prayed over his troops, and later, with a gun in hand, led them into battle."

"The force of evil, sometimes, can be faced no other way. If good men don't stand up for freedom, we will lose it."

"Shooting Indians on the warpath, or killing a man that comes to where you are to kill and rob you is one thing, but we rode one-hundred

James W. Cole

fifty miles chasing these men before the shooting turned to killing. Don't get me wrong, I don't intend to leave without Bessie, I just wonder if we are doing this the right way?"

"Well, consider Daniel Boone, Davy Crockett, family men, and they fought for and stood for freedom. They both traveled great distances for the freedom of others," Pastor Jerry related.

"All right, I suppose there is no stopping anyway. What about a ranch over near Ten Gallon, The Circle G, what do you know about it?"

"Old man Gunther is a hard man," he said, "he's caused a lot of trouble. He has a hard crew working for him, pays them fightin' wages. I'd be very careful if that's who you're dealing with."

"What about Zane Sheridan?" I asked.

"He's a good man, how is he connected?" he asked.

"He has agreed to help."

We talked some more about old times and other things, and then I excused myself as my stomach reminded me that all I had had to eat was a couple of strips of beef jerky and some water. I was almost out the front door when I was jolted in my boots.

Chapter Thirteen

"You! What are you doing in here?" It was a middle aged woman dressed like it was Sunday-go-to-meeting time, all neat and proper. Her hair was done up on top of her head complete with hat. "What are you doing in the church house?"

I was so startled I didn't know what to say.

"You of all people, a killer, in the house of God. You ought to be ashamed of yourself, and with a gun no less."

I looked down at my pistol and back up at her and said, "But Lady--"

"What have you come here to do, mess up the church?"

"Please Lady," I made a step for the door but she blocked it.

"A gun in the church house, what did you do, shoot the pastor?" she asked, her eyes glaring.

I was trying to be polite, but now I'd lost my patience, "woman do you have any money?"

Her mouth flew open and she half slapped the side of her face, "What?" she asked, her breath

James W. Cole

almost gone, "are you going to rob me right here in the church house?"

By this time I was aware that Pastor Jerry was standing near the pulpit listening to us, but he didn't say a word.

"Do you have any money?" I asked again, with a slightly higher more demanding tone.

Her face turned red and she began to dig in her purse.

"I don't want your money, I just wanted to know if you had any. Your money is just like this gun," I patted my Colt as I spoke, "this gun or your money is not good or bad, it's what you do with it that makes it good or bad. You can put your money in this church and it is good, you put it into whiskey, gambling or other corrupt practices, and it is bad."

"I can put this gun in the offering, the pastor can take it and sell it and feed some poor hungry fellow. I use this gun to defend my freedom, and the freedom of others. Either way it's good. I do not rob banks or little old ladies."

"You take the guns away from the good people of the world and the bad folks will take over, sometimes you have to fight fire with fire. So, if you don't mind, I think I'll keep it."

Now it was she that didn't know what to say. She turned and stormed out of the church.

"Well, I never," she said as she hit the bottom step."

Return to the Saddle

I turned and looked at Pastor Jerry, "Don't mind her, she means well," he said, "it just comes out wrong sometimes."

"Care for some fish, I'm hungry," I said.

"Go ahead, I'll catch you later."

❖ ❖ ❖

Mid-afternoon found the Gold Miner's Café almost empty. My bunch was sitting in the back. Maybe we could discuss some plans.

"Hey, Boss Man, we done thought you got lost," Rich blurted out with his southern dialect.

"Yeah," Ron jumped in with a grin, "we thought maybe that Appaloosa throwed you and run off."

"I was down on the Rocking R," I said.

"When are we going home?" Rich asked.

"Yeah, Ron jumped in again, I need some money."

"Just hold your horses," I replied.

"I could use a payday myself, and I'd like to be at home," Rich said with an obvious look of someone ready to go.

"Fellas--," I started.

"I can advance you some money," Jim said.

I flipped a double eagle twenty-dollar gold piece to Ron and one to Rich. Their faces lit up at the sight of the money.

"If you're giving money away, I'll take some," Ben said.

"Need some?" I asked looking at Ben.

James W. Cole

"I was just kidding, I'm all right," he said. Ben always had money. Jim always had money too.

"Boss, we could come back in two or three months and look some more," Rich said.

Joan sat a cup of coffee down in front of me and said, "Fish is almost ready."

"Yeah, let me have one with some taters and a couple of those big cathead biscuits," I said.

"Bossman, I'm ready to go home," Rich said, "my wife and daughter has been too long without me."

"Listen, listen," I said, I lowered my voice a little and continued, "I know where Bessie is."

"Now we're getting somewhere," Ben said.

"Let's go," Ron said as he jumped up. That was his style, throw caution to the wind and take off.

"Sit down Ron," I said, "I promised Sheridan I'd wait 'til morning."

"He going?" Jim asked.

"Yeah, he's going," I answered.

"Good," Jim said with relief, "that mans a fire breathing dragon when it comes to a fight."

As I explained to them what I had discovered and what we wanted to do, Howard brought out my fish. He set my plate down and listened a minute. "I'm going too."

Suddenly, Joan was there with more coffee. "What's going on?" she asked.

"John knows where Bessie is and we're going after her," Ron explained.

"Howard, you and Joan have a job here. Besides, it's not your fight," I said.

Return to the Saddle

"What is a friend if he's not there when you need him?" Howard asked. "Bessie is a little girl," Joan said, "she may need a woman's care when you find her. My sister can take my place while I'm gone."

"My wife can cook in my place," Howard added.

"Well," I looked at Ben, "what can I say? Be ready an hour before daylight and be ready for a fight."

"Sounds good to me," Ben said.

I eased across to the General Store to pick up a new hat. After some looking and considering, I settled on a high crown; it was similar to my old hat, except it had a flat brim, and the color was just right, light tan. Then I slipped off to the Hotel for some rest.

❖ ❖ ❖

At one o'clock in the afternoon the next day, ten of us were on a hill overlooking the Circle G. Sheridan had lead us on a back trail into the main ranch house. It was quiet as we studied the layout.

After we sat quietly and watched the place for some time, Sheridan spoke out, "It won't get any better."

"Probably not," said Marshall Jackson. (Sheridan had asked the Marshall to come along.)

"What do you say we leave one man here, one by the back door of the barn, and the rest take the house quickly? I am counting on the fact that Bessie is a child, they won't fly off the handle and shoot her when we go charging in," Sheridan suggested.

"Sounds good to me," I said, "let Jim stay here with his Sharps rifle. He can strike a match on that fence post down yonder."

"I'll stay in the barn," Rich said.

I thought I was fast and able, but when we started down that hill on foot, Sheridan and Ben were out in front of me. We went down that hill and up behind the barn in a flash.

Rich ran past me and I stuck my head inside. Moments later I heard the wind leave somebody and I stuck my head inside. "Rich, you O.K.?" I asked.

"Everything's fine here, go for the house."

By this time Dale, Howard, Ron, Joan, and Marshall Jackson were all beside the barn. By now everyone was acquainted so Sheridan seemed to naturally take command. He quietly gave more instructions. "Ron, you and the lady go with Dale and Howard down the blind side in a minute and quickly in the back door. The rest of us will give you half a minute and we're going in the front."

Even the Marshall didn't seem to mind following Sheridan. Had I heard he was the General's nephew? No time now to worry about that.

Return to the Saddle

"Hey, Boss man, look a here," Rich spoke from inside the barn.

I looked and he was dragging a canvas off of a nice shiny coach that was stored in the barn.

"Ron, is that the coach you saw by the trail?"

Ron took a long look and said, "Yeah, yeah that's it!"

"Let's go," Sheridan said.

The others raced for the back door, that left four of us heading for the front door. Sheridan didn't wait for anyone. He hit the front porch, grabbed the door open and we poured in.

You could see all the way through the house to the back door and just as we entered the front door, the back door jumped clean off the hinges, flew across the room and landed on the couch.

Dale and Ron both had kicked it and didn't have a choice but to go. Dale grinned and said, "It was locked."

Everyone took off for different rooms of the house, I stayed by the front door. Howard came to the front of the house and was about to enter what looked like a study, when the door opened from the other side.

Howard immediately leveled his shotgun at an old man with gray hair combed straight back. He was tall and strong looking and had a six-gun in his hand, but with one look at the scatter, he forgot about doing anything.

"What are you doing?" he shouted as I grabbed the six-gun from his hand.

"We could ask you the same," I retorted.

James W. Cole

"What's he doing in my house? I don't allow his kind in my house," the old man blurted.

"He's with me," I said at a somewhat higher tone, "besides you're on the wrong end of that Riot gun to be asking such questions."

"I'll have you to know that you are on Circle G Ranch and I'm Robert Gunther, the boss here."

About this time there was a scream in one room and some shouting and arguing in another. The old man made an attempt to move to go toward the scream, but Howard blocked his way.

"Mr. Robert Gunther," I said with some resentment, "we know exactly where we are and what we're doing."

At that moment Ron came from the kitchen with the cook and Joan was right behind him. Sheridan and the Marshall came out with a woman and a small child.

There she was. That was Bessie, the little girl that had stayed and played at my house. I almost jumped to grab her, but I noticed she was sleepy eyed and standing close to the woman.

Dale came in from another part of the house and said, "There's no one else here."

"What do you want?" Gunther asked.

"We came for little Miss Betsy Green," the Marshall announced.

"NO!" the woman shouted. She was a beautiful woman, about thirty and for the first time fear came into her eyes. "You can't have her--she's mine."

"That's my granddaughter. The picture over the mantle, that's proof that she is."

I looked and almost lost my breath.

Chapter Fourteen

"That picture was taken a year ago just before my son-n-law, George, died. You can check the grave marker out yonder. That girl, Lila, is my granddaughter," Gunther shouted.

I looked, even stared at the picture. These girls could have been twins. I slowly pulled the locket out of my pocket and showed Marshall Jackson. It was the first time that he had seen it. There was one good thing about the locket, it was a close-up of the Green family.

"Well, I'll be John Brown!" the Marshall exclaimed.

"I'll not have this," Gunther hollered again, "you bunch of polecats invading my home. Get out or I'll--"

"Hold it!" shouted Ron. His six-gun flew from his holster with lightning speed. Then suddenly everybody was pointing a gun at someone. The cook had come up with a gun from somewhere. Old man Gunther had been standing near a bookcase where a pistol was hidden.

Return to the Saddle

"Go ahead, give me an excuse. I know your kind, you run over everybody," Ron shouted, "farmers, settlers, small ranchers, and anyone that gets in your way."

It was a miracle that no one fired a shot.

"Hold it, Ron," Marshall Jackson ordered, "I'm the law here and I'll handle this. Put your gun away."

By this time Gunther and his cook realized they didn't have a chance and threw down their guns. Ron and the rest of us responded by putting ours away.

"Gunther, do you have any real proof that this is your granddaughter? Colter, do you have any real proof that this is the Green girl?" the Marshall quizzed.

I walked over to the picture on the wall. I looked closely. Then I saw a large freckle, or a mole as some call it, on the cheek of the girl in the picture.

"There is a mole on Gunther's granddaughter," I pointed to the picture, "there are no spots on Bessie anywhere, and how did you know who Betsy Green was?"

Everybody looked and began to mumble.

"It fell off about six months ago," the woman said.

"My daughter, Roberta, has gone through enough with the loss of her husband, you can't take her daughter," Gunther shouted as he paced the room, "Lila is her daughter."

James W. Cole

"I suggest sir," Sheridan spoke for the first time," that the fever that came through here last year and killed George, also took your granddaughter."

Everybody in the house had a look of surprise on their face. Apparently no one in our bunch knew this except Sheridan. Jim Wester might have known but he was up on the Ridge.

Suddenly, the front door jumped open and a man came through and said, "hold it."

Dale was standing behind the door. He quickly knocked the six-gun from his hand and slapped him so hard, with his Winchester, that he sailed across the room, hit a big heavy chair, and knocked it over backwards and fell with it.

Sheridan quickly ducked out the door. Howard was right behind him. We knew there would be more.

I drew my six-gun and ran over to the man on the floor. He was out cold and would be there for a while. We were not getting anywhere fast, and the longer we stayed here the less chances of getting out.

I slipped my Colt back in my holster. The others were whispering among themselves. I knew this had to be resolved soon or we would be in trouble, despite the Marshall being with us.

I walked part way across the room toward the woman and the child. "Bessie, your mom and dad sent me for you." Fear shown in her eyes. She didn't respond to me, but stood close to the woman.

Return to the Saddle

"Don't be afraid honey, everything's all right," I said.

"Leave her alone," the woman said, hate now beginning to show in her face and eyes, "she's just a child."

"Bessie, do you remember staying at my home and playing with my daughter and our little baby boy?" Her eyes brightened and she spoke for the first time, "Marie--Benny?"

"Yes," I said and dropped to one knee, "come on baby and let's go home." I held my arms out and she broke away from the woman and ran to me. I grabbed her up and turned toward the door.

The woman moved to stop us and Joan spun her around and threw her into a chair and said, "Sit down!"

The cook and old man Gunther made a move at the same time to stop me, Ron whacked the old man on the head with his pistol barrel and Dale slapped the cook with the stock of his rifle.

We didn't wait to see what else would happen. We ran for the barn and found there had been two riders.

"Got the drop on me bossman," Rich said. "Sheridan handled him real good though. Came in the front door yonder and threw an ear of corn in the window of the coach, making all kinds of racket and as the man turned to look, Sheridan cold-cocked him from behind."

"Are there any more here?" I asked.

"Marshall, Ron, Joan, and myself will take Bessie and go if you want the rest of the men to help you make an arrest," I suggested.

"I want to find Lila's grave, or whatever happened to her first. Durbin and I will come back later," he said.

Ben had been quiet most of the day, but now he spoke, "folks, I don't want to be pushy, but I suggest we go while we can. This bunch can be pretty tough."

"He's right, we both just barely made it out of here before. Let's go," I said.

We climbed the hill and found Jim had another man tied up. We hastened our departure even more, knowing this thing could blow up any minute.

Joan and Bessie took to each other right away. It was easy to see Joan loved children. Bessie seemed to be at ease with her.

The horses had rested only about two hours. They were probably not ready for the return ride to Virginia City. An eight-hour ride to get there was enough without asking them to ride all the way back.

Nevertheless, we mounted up and hit the trail. It was almost dark when we stopped. Sheridan found a secluded spot for us to make a dry camp. It was mostly surrounded by rocks, although we could get out quickly if we needed to.

Bessie seemed to be at ease. She kept an eye on me as if she would be lost without me.

Return to the Saddle

I walked over just to reassure her. "Bessie are you all right?" I asked, "Sweetheart, we're going home soon."

"Yes sir," she answered, "I'm so glad."

"We haven't had time to stop and we may not be able to stay here long. Joan is a good friend and you can rest here with her okay?"

"Yes, sir, I'll be all right," she said.

"You're a brave girl, soon we'll be home with Ma and Pa," I said, trying to reassure her.

"She's a good girl," Joan said, "we are doing fine."

"All right, get some rest," I said and turned to the chores at hand.

No one rested for very long. The uneasiness of the Circle G hands possibly catching up to us made everyone want to be back in Virginia City.

With about two hours sleep, we mounted up and slowly rode on into the Comstock. The old Indians had called it the Washoe. A mining town that had settled down some in the last few years and perhaps had scaled down a bit.

It was almost dawn and Sheridan had excused himself before we hit town. Marshall Jackson did the same as we entered town.

The rest would sleep an hour or two and some of us would sleep longer. Howard and Joan would probably work today.

Chapter Fifteen

I awakened with a start. What was that: I sprang to a sitting position in the bed. Then there was another shot. I grabbed my pistol and stepped to the window of the hotel where we were staying.

It was just some drunken cowboy letting off a little steam. I lowered my six-gun, lowered the curtain to its natural position and breathed a sigh of relief.

Sometimes it happened like this. I would wake up with a start and not know where I was going or what was going on. I turned hot for a moment and then began to settle down. I took a deep breath of air and began to think.

Bessie was at Joan's sister's house playing with their kids. Ron, Rich, Ben, and Jim were all somewhere in town, everything should be fine.

I had slept with my clothes on as I sometimes did when I had little time. I shook my boots out and stopped to think again. That uneasy feeling would not leave. I looked at my watch, it was almost noon. I had slept longer than I thought. I

Return to the Saddle

pulled on my boots, grabbed my new hat and my gun and out the door I went.

I knocked on Ben's room door next to mine. I straightened my vest and waited a moment. No answer. I stepped down to the next room and knocked on the door. I pulled my hat off, pushed my hair back, slipped the new hat back on and took off.

Where was everybody? I went down the stairs two at a time and was almost out the door when I heard somebody say, "Hey, Mr Colter."

I turned to look back and saw the hotel clerk. The short, skinny and baldheaded fella with a mustache was standing behind the desk grinning at me.

"The others said to tell you they would be at the Gold Miner's Café when you came down," he said.

"Thanks a lot," I replied and saluted him with two fingers and out the door I went. I was in deep thought about what might be going on in the café and didn't see the horse and rider bearing down on me.

Suddenly I noticed someone standing on the sidewalk waving their arms frantically, then I noticed the young boy was saying, "Look out for the horse!"

I didn't want to look, I just took off running and put one hand on the side of the horse watering trough and swung over behind it and fell flat on my back.

James W. Cole

The horse and rider ran by at high speed just as I ducked behind the trough. I rolled over and said, "Thanks, I--"

Suddenly a shot hit the top of the trough. Water splashed out on me. I fell back and jerked my hand away from the top of the trough. Another shot splashed even more water out on me.

Then I heard the horse drawing closer. Gun in hand, I knew I would have but one slim chance and I would have to pick the best spot. Where were Ben and the others? Surely they were close enough to notice what was going on.

A shot rang out and I felt the bullet tear at my vest on the left side, as my right side was drawn up tight against the trough. I threw the barrel of my pistol over the top of the trough and shot at the sound of his gun. It was probably high as I didn't want to risk shooting an innocent bystander.

Just then I heard the sound of a whip. The sharp crack of the whip and then the groan of a man, perhaps the sound a pistol as it hit the ground, or was it the horse stamping the ground.

Now! Now was the time. Go! I jumped to my feet and faced the street. The gunman had lost his pistol to the whip, but now was struggling to pull a rifle from the saddle holster. The horse had wiggled past the watering trough and down by the boy's wagon by which he was huddled underneath.

I jumped, my left foot on the trough, then my right to the back of the wagon, and then over the side of the wagon about the time he was about to

Return to the Saddle

bring the rifle to bare. I dove and hit him chest to chest, knocking him out of the saddle.

His rifle went sailing out into the street. I rolled and came up on my feet. His move was slower because he jarred the ground hard. As he rolled over and came to one knee, I kicked him in the forehead. He flipped over backward and hit the ground again.

By this time everyone was there. Ben and the others, as well as the Marshall. "What's going on here?" the Marshall demanded. "Put that gun away," he directed at me.

I still had the Colt in my hand so I slipped it in my holster. "Marshall, this man dry gulched me," I explained.

"That's right," the boy said as he climbed out from under the wagon. "He tried to run him down and when that ain't work he tried to shoot 'em," his broken English obvious.

"Marshall, it's jest as the kid sez." I looked around to a man about my age speaking. My eyes dropped to his hands and I saw the whip.

By now the would be killer was struggling to his feet. I stepped over and grabbed him by the shirt. "Who sent you?" I demanded, rather roughly.

The Marshall stepped between us. "I'll handle this," he said. He then grabbed the gunner and hauled him off.

As I stood looking, Ben stepped up and asked, "Are you all right?"

"Yeah, I'm fine," I answered still staring at the Marshall and his prisoner.

"We came to the café door and looked one time. All we saw was this cowboy acting silly, so we didn't look anymore," Ben explained.

"Yeah," I said, "I looked from the hotel window too, and didn't think much of it either." I was still staring at the Marshall and his prisoner. "I wonder?"

Suddenly, the owlhoot turned on the Marshall and jammed his shoulder into him, grabbed the Marshall's gun and turned on me again. With blazing speed, that I never could figure out where it came from, I drew and fired twice.

He hit the ground so fast that I couldn't tell where I hit him. We ran over to see. One bullet in the stomach, the other in the shoulder. He was still alive. "Get a doctor," I yelled to the crowd.

The crowd was buzzing. Someone took off after the doctor. The Marshall, sheepishly, climbed to his feet. He looked at me and said, "Sorry."

The kid ran over and put a hand on my shoulder as I knelt to examine the wounded man. "Hey, I ain't never seen nobody so fast!" he exclaimed with an excited grin on his face.

I looked past the boy to his dad. His dad didn't say anything, so I looked at Ben. "Young man," Ben said, "this really is not very funny."

"But he was so fast," the boy offered.

"I can't draw on a tin can near as fast," I said, "something about the danger changes things."

The doctor arrived and we stepped back.

The Marshall eased over and said, "Don't worry about it. If he makes it I'll try to find out

Return to the Saddle

who sent him." He then turned and walked away, not waiting on a comment from me or the doctor.

"Hey kid," I said, "thanks for helping me out." I reached to shake his hand and he grabbed my hand and shook it with fast up and down movement.

"Nothin' to it," he said, "glad to shake the fastest hand in the West."

I then turned to the boy's dad, "Thanks Mister, your whip saved my bacon," I said, trying to make things seem a little lighter.

He reached out and shook my hand and said, "I never leave a man in a heap of trouble when it wattin' his doin'."

"Can I buy you dinner?" I asked, "it's the least I can do for what you and this young man did for me."

"No, thanks anyhow," the man said, "we got them supplies loaded and we're headed for Sacramentie. Was jest about to shove off when all the commotion started."

❖ ❖ ❖

They bid us farewell and started on their way. A few minutes later Jim, Ben, Ron, Rich, and myself were seated at our usual table by the front window, sipping coffee and discussing the recent events.

"He didn't just accidentally pick you to shoot John," Ben said.

"I agree," Jim said, "somebody sent him."

"That's what I thought all along," I added.

James W. Cole

I pushed my chair back a little and pulled my pistol out and pointed it toward the floor and reloaded it. I was a little miffed that I had waited so long.

"Jim, do you have a load for Ron's wagon? We need to be on our way before anything else happens," I said, feeling some discomfort over the whole matter.

"Yeah, as a matter of fact, I do. It's sittin' in the warehouse just waitin' on you," Jim said.

"Let's load it before dark so we can be out of here before daylight in the morning, we can't wait any longer on the Marshall to draw up a case on the old man," I said.

"Haven't you heard," Jim asked, " a judge over there close to the old man has already dismissed any charges connected to Bessie or us; we are on our own."

"Let's load that wagon and leave right after dark. We can have twenty miles behind us by daylight," I said.

"I am going," a soft voice said.

I looked up to see Joan speaking as she poured our coffee.

"Bessie still needs a woman's care. My sister can work in my place till I get back."

I looked at Ron, searching for an answer.

"Well, load your gun and pack your bag honey," Ron said with a sparkle in his eyes.

No one knew what to say. If we kept sitting around, some hired gun-man the old man hired

Return to the Saddle

off the street might get too close, then where would we be?

❖ ❖ ❖

By dark-thirty we were rolling. We took a back way out of town, picked Bessie up at Joan's sister's house, and kept going. Jim offered to come along and bring one or two of his men, but I wouldn't let him. There was a chance we could be too far gone before anyone knew.

"Mr. John," Bessie called to me as I rode alongside the wagon. Ron had the reins and Joan was sitting by his side. Bessie was on the end of the seat next to me.

"Yes, Miss Bessie," I said.

"Mr. John are we going home?"

"Yes, sweetheart, we are on our way," I answered.

"Is Ma and Pa going to be there?"

Then it dawned on me that Bessie may have been told a lot of bad things about her Mom and Pop.

"Sweetheart, your Ma and Pa love you very much. They will be so glad to see you. Your Pa wanted to come, but I wouldn't let him. He wasn't very easy to talk into staying behind. But you don't worry, honey child, we'll throw a party and celebrate your being at home."

Joan put her arm around Bessie and said, "They are saving everything for you Bessie, your bed at home, your place at the table, your seat at

James W. Cole

school, and your place at Church, it's all there waiting for you."

"Really?" Bessie quizzed and smiled as she looked up at Joan.

I could see that Joan was right. Bessie needed a woman's touch. I could also see that Ron had better marry this woman while he had the chance, she was a fine lady. She was a good waitress, but she would be a better wife and mother.

Ben was the only one that didn't know this trail well enough to travel it blind-folded. Rich, Ron, and myself had crossed it with a team of mules many times.

❖ ❖ ❖

We slept about two hours just before daylight and by late afternoon we had started the climb up the mountain. We had pushed the mules and horses really hard and we would soon have to break for the night and give it a rest.

Ben had been riding drag and had chopped off a leafy limb and brushed out our trail in two or three different places. This would not hold them for long, but any little bit helped. I tried to hold on to some bit of hope that they wouldn't come. Somehow, though, that didn't give me any comfort.

I dropped back as Ben caught up with us. "Ben, we're going to have to rest the mules before long. Maybe we will be closer to the top in another hour. There are several places up there that would offer

Return to the Saddle

good shelter," I spoke hoping we would make it to the top.

"Well, I don't know what it means, but I saw a cloud of dust rising up several miles back. If they are after us, they will catch us before long," Ben said with a hint of concern in his voice.

"Tell you what, let's prepare for the worst and if it comes we'll be ready. Spread the word and I'll drop back and see. If it's them, I'll try to slow them down," I said and turned to ride.

"Be careful," Ben warned, with the same concern.

As Banjo broke into a trot, I double checked all of my guns as I also watched the trail that we had just came across. The Winchester, the Colt, and the derringer in my vest pocket were all ready to go.

I knew if I rode very far out into the flat it would be harder to hide, so I picked a place after a mile or two, to stop and wait. An hour passed before I saw them coming. The Gray of Dusk was settling in.

Standing under the shade of a small tree, so there would be no glints of sunlight bouncing off of the guns or field glasses, I stood and observed through the lens until I was sure. Yes, there was the old man in the bunch, and three of the hands I saw on the ranch, about twenty in all. There must not be anyone left on the ranch but the young woman. No matter, here and now this twenty was the concern.

I walked over to Banjo and started to pull the rifle, then I thought, one or two would be all I would get before they would be on me. If I stood under this little tree and tried to pick ' em off. They would drop to the ground for cover and I would not get any more good shots.

❖ ❖ ❖

Suddenly, I jammed the rifle back into the boot and jumped on Banjo. If I ride out now they might not see me. I'll look for a better place up on the side of the mountain. By now the wagon should be over halfway to the top.

"Lord, help me to make it," I spoke aloud the prayer that I had prayed many times, 'in Jesus name', that was the only way. This deal did not look good. Four men, a woman and a child, against twenty men. This was not too good.

I stopped two or three times as I started up the mountain to see how they were doing. They were coming on hard, and my stopping to look and think allowed them to gain on me. I crossed the Truckee River three times as the trail switched from side to side and was now stopped again. For a moment I remembered the times I had stopped to observed the beauty of this mountain, the clear water, the tall pines, and the huge rocks. The thought was brief as I heard them coming below.

I looked back, then ahead, then I saw it. The trail ahead narrowed and there were rocks and trees on both sides of the road. I clucked and Banjo

Return to the Saddle

jumped and shortly I was at the spot. I grabbed my rope, jumped down, and slapped Banjo on the rump and he took off.

I ran across, tied the rope to a tree, stretched it across the road, and quickly covered it with a few leaves. With the loose end of the rope, I dropped behind a tree and a small rock. It wasn't but a minute until they were there. I jerked the rope up and pulled it tight.

I was a second early, but in the shadows they didn't see the rope until it was too late. They were riding hard and close and piled in on the rope hard. There were men yelling, horses groaning, and a big mess. I held on tight to the rope.

Suddenly the rope broke. I didn't hesitate one second, I threw it down and turned to run. I ran across an opening toward some more trees. I had made about one hundred fifty feet when a shot rang out. Dust flew up at my feet and I dove for cover behind some trees.

I whipped out my six-gun, and fired three quick shots in their direction and took off again. This time I had the last clump of trees and darkness between me and them. I sailed over a hump and downhill I ran, back into the road. I hoped to catch up with my horse, but he was nowhere in sight.

I ran up the trail and was about to make the next river crossing when more shots rang out. Something slipped out from under my right foot and I fell, right straight into the water-and boy it was cold. The current was strong, so I stayed under water as long as I could and swam downstream.

I came up for air and quickly looked around, I couldn't see anything. The current was still carrying me downstream. Quickly I swam to the far side of the river. I could walk up the narrow ledges where the river came close to the mountain wall. I stopped briefly to check myself out. No wounds or bullet holes anywhere, what happened? No matter, I had to go. I began to run, the water squeaked in my boots, even though I had tried to get most of it out.

I had gone passed the spot where I fell and hoped I was passed the old man and his crew. I slowed to a walk so I could be as sure as possible. My hat was gone, and my six-gun was gone too. I had to catch up to the others or at least my horse.

❖ ❖ ❖

Suddenly a cowboy jumped out in front of me. I realized too late that it was one of them. How he got this far ahead I didn't know.

"Hold it right there, Mr. Colter," he spoke with an air of satisfaction, "I don't think you be gettin' away mite so easy this time."

I stopped and was completely still for a moment. Then I realized that I was standing in a much darker spot than he was. I slowly began to reach for my vest. As he was talking and being so proud of himself--he was mumbling something about collecting $1000 for nailing me--I thought

Return to the Saddle

of those in Sacramento, the Green's, my wife and kids. Would I make it back, would Bessie be returned home? Never quit, I thought.

My hand was in the vest pocket. The Derringer was there. The owlhoot was so sure of himself, he had only taken one or two steps toward me. He had not even bothered to say 'raise your hands'. Was my Derringer dry enough to fire? If not I could be a dead duck.

I thumbed the Derringer and fired, then fired again. He just stood there motionless. I couldn't see the expression on his face. It gave me a sickening feeling. I hated this, but if I had warned him in any way, he would have shot me first. I had to get going before the rest of his bunch caught up. I slowly stepped to my right three or four steps.

"You can't get away," he said somewhat hollow. There was a moments hesitation. He had never cocked his gun. I made two more steps to my right. Then I saw he was not following me and I took two more steps and quickly reloaded my Derringer.

"You shot me," he said and he dropped to his knees, then fell on his face.

"You picked the wrong crowd to run with," I said, as though he heard me. I didn't bother to check him. I just took off again, softly running, trying to put some distance between me and them.

Suddenly, I tripped over something and through the air I sailed and hit the ground. I don't remember anything being here. Laying still

James W. Cole

and quiet could be a mistake, but I didn't move. After a moment with no sounds I climbed to my feet and walked back.

It was just a limb that had fallen in the road. I was insulted at myself that I let such a thing happen. I turned to go on up the trail, much slower and more cautious this time.

❖ ❖ ❖

It was on into the night when I caught up to the others. It was still quiet a ways to the top. I stopped outside the camp and stood listening to see what was inside the camp.

"Come on in John," Ben's welcome voice reached me. I had not stood there but a minute when he called.

I stepped out and walked on in to the dark.

"Ben how did you know it was me?" I asked.

"Man during the war you learned to know or get killed," he answered.

"Well, I sometimes think I can slip up on an Apache, but you beat all," I said, amazed.

"I had the privilege of serving under Robert E. Lee. That man was a gentleman, a scholar, and a General, a real leader. If you wanted to learn you would if you stayed around him."

"Well I'll say," I said, surprised, "I thought I knew a lot about your war experience."

"Where have you been?" Ben asked pointedly.

Return to the Saddle

"I went for a swim, and you know I went in the other way in that strong current. I also ran into one of their guys and just barely got away."

"I looked for you high and low. I even saw what a mess you made for them."

"How many are down?" I asked.

"Ah, seven or eight maybe."

"Did you see Banjo?" I asked.

"Yeah, that's how I knew to look for you."

"Find yourself a blanket, I'll watch a while," he said.

"O.K." I said, "by the way, how could you tell it was me?"

"If a man thinks he's among friends, he moves with a little more ease. If he thinks he's close to an enemy his steps are very slow and cautious!" Ben exclaimed.

"I didn't think I made a sound."

"You didn't," he said, "you follow the pattern of birds, crickets, and other animals, how quickly they quiet down, and how far their pattern of quietness goes."

"There are some things that have become easy for me, like Ron over there woke up as soon as you said something. He's asleep again now that he knows I'm here and he never moved," I said.

"Yeah," Ben said, "his lady friend woke up too and she's still awake."

Ben was amused but kept it quiet. "Well I knew where they bedded down. She's on the back side of the camp with Bessie."

"O.K. Good night," I said.

I found Banjo tied up in back of the camp. A quick search of my saddle bags and I found my spare pistol. I quietly checked and loaded it and checked my rifle in the saddle boot, and found a place to bed down.

I didn't sleep but about four hours and was up again. This time Rich was on guard. It irritated me that I didn't know when they changed. Was it because they were my friends?

"It's quiet," Rich said, "they won't try anything 'til they lick their wounds."

"Yeah," I said kind of flatly.

I pulled my long knife from my boot, propped my foot on the big rock Rich was standing behind and quietly began to rub it across the top of my leather boot to fine-tone the cutting edge.

"My Pa said 'that knife won't be sharp when Gabriel blows the trumpet'," I remarked. "He didn't think much of my knife, but I picked it for two reasons: I thought it would last, and it would fit inside my boot. And it has served the purpose."

"You thought a lot of your Pa, didn't you?" Rich asked.

"Yeah, I did. Not at first though. When I was younger, I didn't think he cared, but later I saw quite clearly that he loved me very much."

"Yeah it's funny how that goes sometimes," Rich replied.

Chapter Sixteen

It was just breaking dawn and Ben eased up behind me. We remained quiet for a moment, then he said, "They're on their way."

"I'll wake the others," Rich said.

"They're awake," I said.

Soon we began to see a little dust stirring down the road. Ben began to quietly tell the others what to do and where to get. I had known this man only since we had been in Sacramento, but not a better friend did I have. We knew each other well, as though the time had been much longer. I was completely at ease with his leadership.

We settled down behind cover and it wasn't long until we all knew they were close.

Then suddenly from out of the rocks came the old man's voice, "One last chance Colter, give up the girl and we let you live."

I knew what my answer was without thought, but I just waited. Ben looked at me from about twenty feet away and pointed to where he was in

James W. Cole

one direction and then indicated for me to take one bunch and he'd take the other.

Bessie began to cry lightly, but Joan quickly comforted her. She must have thought my not answering meant I was thinking about giving her back.

Then the old man shouted again, "Everyone dies Colter, nobody escapes!"

I had hoped by not answering him that he would not be sure where we were, giving us the early edge.

Then it broke loose. They began firing in all directions because they didn't know where we were. We were all watching Ben, he was holding his hand out about a foot above the ground, like he was pushing air to the ground. I had never seen a strategy of wait like this. He must have known they wouldn't move. We had everything well hidden-horses, packs, wagon, and ourselves as well.

It seemed like a long time that we waited and they had not gotten a shot close. Then Ben gave the signal and popped up just far enough to fire. We all did the same.

I popped up and began to fire, in the direction Ben indicated, with my Winchester. About two hundred feet away I saw three of them standing well above cover.

Just the two minutes of waiting had made them relax and had probably caught them reloading. I rapidly fired one shot a piece at each of them.

Return to the Saddle

Two went down, the other ducked for cover and so did I.

It was just then that the top of the rock splintered with shots fired at me. I moved down the rock a little and came up firing again. I emptied my rifle and ducked again.

I looked over at Ben just as he looked at me. I held up two fingers and he held up three. I looked at the others, Rich was firing with his left handed pistol, Ron was too. They probably had already emptied their rifles and immediately grabbed their pistols.

They were both hot headed, yet cautious. Gunther's guys were returning their fire, too. I quickly reloaded, five down and seven to go? Couldn't count on it.

I scooted over to another rock and peeped around the left corner. One was running right at me, I leaned way out to get a clear shot and cut him down. Then shots hit all around me as I fell back behind the rock. That was crazy, but it worked.

Just as I fell back I saw one of the owlhoots slip in the side of our camp. I leveled my rifle and fired, but not before he shot Rich in the back. They both went down at the same time.

I ran to Rich and dropped to his side. I breathed a sigh of relief, it was only a flesh wound on the inside of his arm. I grabbed my neckerchief and tied it off and said, "It's all right Rich, no big deal."

I grabbed his pistol and started to reload it and he reached for it and said, "I got it bossman, go on."

Was it seven down and five to go, or had some survived the rope the evening before? Chances are high that some were patched up out there and were shooting at us. I held low and scooted back to my place.

❖ ❖ ❖

Suddenly the shooting stopped. I looked at Ben, then around our camp. What was going on? The man I shot was still laying where he fell over next to Rich. What were they doing? I watched and listened closely. They didn't seem to be doing anything.

I checked and reloaded my guns. I peered out toward the one I had shot in the open flat. He was gone! It was a direct hit, but where was he?

Ben slid over next to me and quietly said, "They dragged your friend off out there, but it was too late for him."

"When?" I asked, puzzled.

"While you were over by Rich," he said.

"They are trying to regroup," he said, "In about fifteen minutes they'll come again."

"Don't you think they've had enough?"

"Nope, the old man's too stubborn."

"Yeah, you're right," I agreed.

"Let's hit 'em right now, just me and you," Ben said, surprising me greatly.

Return to the Saddle

"What?" I asked, shocked.

"Let Ron move over to your spot quickly and let's go before we lose the edge," Ben poked back at me with more intensity, "Behind the lines of guerrilla warfare. This is a fort here, they can hold it. We will have the element of surprise!"

My heart began to pump faster. I had done this before back in the wagon train and in Indian battles, but with different odds.

I jumped and moved Ron to my spot. Ben was already gone. I darted out the side of our camp in the same place the dead outlaw had came in. Moving low and fast I stopped only briefly to read the set in front of me.

With quickness and quietness of a Blackfoot Indian, I moved through the shady and low areas to keep from being seen. I had covered about two hundred feet when I stopped again to look and listen. It was about this time that I heard Ben's Henry Repeater bark out with rapid fire.

Ben liked that Henry. He had said 'with some adjustments it was a fine rifle'. Why, he could totally rebuild it so it wasn't the same rifle.

Then right in front of me two men jumped up looking in Ben's direction. I threw down on them quickly with my Winchester. I knew if I covered Ben I would have to move quickly; plus, if I didn't we would lose the element of surprise. Two shots and they were both down.

I took off immediately so they wouldn't get a fix on my position. I quietly darted in behind what looked like a good spot for the rest of them to be.

Suddenly there was someone right in front of me. I threw my rifle around just as he did the same. Then I saw it was Ben. He saw me too and we pulled our rifles back.

He quickly looked at me and pointed over the rock and held up four fingers and gave the motion to go. He ran around the left side of the rock, I ran around to the right side. They realized we were on them and turned to shoot. I pulled the trigger but my reliable Winchester misfired for the first time ever.

I don't know how I did it so fast, but I turned my rifle loosed with my right hand and came out with my replacement pistol and shot the cowboy on the right once, the one on the left twice and again the one on the right once more before they went down.

There were two on Ben's side that I turned to cover, but Ben had pumped them full of lead with his Henry.

"Let's go," Ben said as he ran by me.

I fell in behind him wondering how many more there was. I jacked the shell out of my Winchester and reloaded it as we darted through the trees and rocks, Ben was leading back to our camp. I quickly reloaded my pistol as we went.

We slid in low and went in the side of the camp. We immediately saw fear in everyone's face and we looked to see the old man kneeling down beside Bessie with a pistol to her side.

Chapter Seventeen

"I'll kill her if I can't have her," Gunther threatened.

My stomach sank with a painful, empty feeling. He was mighty close to her to risk a shot. Everyone seemed to have their guns pointed to the ground in an effort to relax this man.

Then suddenly Bessie bit his hand and jumped away from him as he loosened his hold. My rifle was down, so I grabbed my pistol and fired twice. The whole camp vibrated with gunfire as everyone else there did the same.

You could see the old man's shirt rip to shreds as the bullets hit him. He didn't flinch, just simply fell over backwards. He was obviously dead before he hit the ground.

Bessie screamed with much terror in her voice. She had ended up in a heap about twenty feet from the old man in a clump of grass. I holstered my pistol and dropped my rifle as I ran to Bessie. I grabbed her up and held her close as she sobbed uncontrollably. She was near losing her breath in between sobs.

"It's O.K. honey," I kept reassuring her. She was not physically hurt, but she was scared half to death.

Joan ran over to Bessie, grabbed her and held her tightly. "I'm here baby, I'm here," Joan said as she rocked Bessie side to side to console her. I stroked her hair as I stood close by. The others began to gather around.

Suddenly Ron asked, "Where's Rich?"

We turned to look, but didn't see him. Then we scattered and began looking for our friend frantically.

"Be careful," Ben cautioned, "this may not be over."

I picked up my rifle and worked my way past the outer edge of our camp. I was careful as I moved through the rocks and trees, so I wouldn't expose myself to any gunfire.

Then I saw him, and became sick. I ran to where he was lying, knowing it was too late. Rich was lying face down with a knife stuck in his back. I almost lost my breath. Here was a long time friend, dead because he followed my orders. How could I live with that? How could I tell his wife and daughter.

Ben slipped up behind me and put his hand on my shoulder, "I'm sorry friend. It must have happened while we were out of camp."

"We made the best choice we could," I answered.

Return to the Saddle

"The old man died like he lived," Ben continued, "Everyone in our camp must have shot him at least once. If you live by the sword, you die by the sword. We must not look back. The price of freedom is not always free. I saw many die in the Civil War fighting for what they honestly thought was right."

Then I saw it. There was a note stuck in Rich's hand. I pulled it out and read it, "This is just the first. I am sworn to kill the girl's Ma and Pa and as many others as I can--Foreman-Circle G."

"I am sorry Rich is gone," Ben sympathized.

"Look," I turned and handed the note to Ben. He read it and turned and walked off a few steps, obviously deep in thought. I had a hard time just thinking. Here was a man, lying dead at my feet, that I had known my whole life. I had gone to school with him, and moved west with him. He was my first hired hand with the wagons in Sacramento.

I sat down on a nearby rock and put my head in my hands, and just tried to breathe. I wanted to find a hole and crawl in it and never come back.

"John," Ben had returned, "We just don't have time to mourn. One of us has to saddle and ride. Someone has to beat this man to Sacramento or get word to them or something."

I stood up in response to his challenge. "Yes, you are right, I'll go. If you will take care of things here. I'll be in Sacramento in twenty-four hours."

"You'll kill that App tryin'," he said.

"He'll have to make it," I replied.

"Take the big black for a spare. I'll ride in the wagon."

"O.K. Ben," I said, "I'll do it."

I gave Bessie a big hug and told her that I would see her at home, she cried again. It broke my heart to leave, but I couldn't ask anyone else to do my job for me. We had already lost one life.

In thirty minutes time I had both horses and was gone. It wasn't long until I started down from the top and the running was easier.

"Lord, help me to make it," I made the simple request as I rode. Two hours later I had covered about twelve miles. Banjo was holding up pretty good as I would step down and lead him uphill. The uphill was slow but there wasn't that much and the downhill was much faster and longer.

Some downhill drops were fairly long and steep. It was easy for the horses to carry me down these long grades. I swapped to Ben's black and then later back to Banjo.

Then later in the day I saw something off to the side of the road. I slowed a little trying to make out what it was. It was beginning to look like somebody. I slowed Banjo to a walk, turning in the saddle, looking in every direction, wary of a trap.

As I began to get close enough to see I realized that this was the young boy from Virginia City that was under the wagon when his dad jerked the gun out of that jokers hand with his whip.

Return to the Saddle

I eased up to where he was and stopped. He just sat there on a rock with his head in his hands not moving.

"Hey son," I addressed him, "Are you all right?"

"No," he answered with a quiver in his voice.

I stepped down and let the reins drop to the ground. I moved to him and put one hand on my knee and the other on his shoulder.

"What's the matter?" I asked. I looked around again as I waited on his answer. All I could see was a small bundle laying on the ground beside him. There was no sign of a wagon, his Pa or anything. I waited, but no answer.

"Where is your Pa, son?" I asked, "Tell me what's happened."

"He's dead," he said quietly, "Something spooked the horses. He told me to jump, I did, and--and he went off to the side of the mountain. He was killed, the horses were killed, the wagon busted all to pieces, and nothing left but what I have here."

"Oh my, I'm so sorry son," I sympathized, "that must have been awful. I wonder if it was those varmits from the Circle G?"

"I don't have anybody anymore," he said, "he was the last kin I had left."

I raised up and began to pace back and forth, thinking about what to do. I needed to be riding hard and fast. The bad guys had struck again and were on their way to Sacramento to kill Bessie's

James W. Cole

Ma and Pa and who knows who else, And here I was standing side of the road.

I didn't even know how many I was chasing, and I was trying hard just to breathe again. I needed both horses to catch up, and if I didn't sleep tonight, I just might make it. I knew the trail well enough to make good time at night and that should be the advantage I would have over the bad guys. That is, if I were alone.

"I don't see anything, where did all of this happen?" I asked.

"Back down the road, I don't know, somewhere. I just started walking after I buried my Pa in a ditch, I caved off some dirt on him."

There was no question as to what I had to do. I couldn't put it off any longer either, the bad guys had too much of a head start on me. I grabbed his bundle and started strapping it to the back of Ben's saddle on the big Black. The fourteen year old boy didn't seem to care what I was doing.

"Climb on board and let's go," I instructed.

"What?" he asked with a funny look on his face.

"Look John Paul, I can't leave you and I don't have time to talk about it, I need you to get on that black horse. Grab those reins and keep up. I don't have time to play."

"I never rode a horse before. We always lived in town and Pa always drove the wagon."

"Well just get up there, hold the reins with a little slack in them and he will do the rest. That's a mighty good horse and you will do just fine

Return to the Saddle

with him," I spoke as politely as I could under the circumstances.

We rode quietly for the next two hours, then darkness began to fall. The elevation was dropping and the downhill pace was good. The pine trees were noticeably shorter, but we didn't have time to stop and enjoy the beauty. The Sierra's were so beautiful, I had often thought of moving here, building a home, and staying. The business and other things had carried me somewhere else.

There was an old stage stop ahead that the man had turned into a small ranch and trading post after the stage line stopped coming through. Maybe we could pick up another horse, some hats and some grub. We needed supplies to make it on in.

It was quiet as we rode in. There were a few horses tied up front, but a quick check of the brands showed no Circle-G stock. We tied our horses and went inside.

"Howdy, partner," the old gent behind the counter spoke as we approached.

"Hey neighbor," I spoke in return.

"What'll you have?" he asked.

"Something quick to eat, coffee to drink, maybe a couple of hats, and a spare horse if you have one."

"Well, let's see, we have beef stew, plenty of coffee, some hats, but as far as the horse, all we have is a mare that has been worked today. I could let you have her for twenty dollars."

"I'll take the whole package. That horse is probably not any worse off than what we have. We've got to be in Sacramento tomorrow."

"You got it," he said.

As I was paying him for everything a cowboy stood up from a table and started toward the counter.

"Us mountain folk don't like you city slickers buying our good horses," he said.

I just ignored him, and picked up my cup of coffee and tested it. Good coffee, I thought.

"I'm talking to you," he said. Then he lunged at me. I threw the hot coffee from the cup right into his face. It stopped him right in his tracks. I calmly placed the cup on the counter and turned and punched him right in the chin before he could recover. He went down, but started to get up. I caught a movement from the table where he was sitting and very suddenly my six-gun was in my hand, hammer cocked and a very mean look popped up on my face.

"If you fellows want to live, you had better forget what you came here for and scat out the door." I stepped to the window and peeked through the curtain to see if they actually left or not. They mounted up and rode west. I watched until they were out of sight in the darkness.

"Here's that stew," the old gent spoke as he set the bowl on the counter.

"I'm very sorry, sir," I apologized, "I didn't mean to make a mess."

Return to the Saddle

"Don't worry about it, here's some more coffee, enjoy your supper. Me and Pedro will straighten up."

"Wow! That was fast!" John Paul exclaimed, "I just can't believe it. I am going to be living with the fastest gun in the west." I just looked at him and the post keeper and grinned, and just shook my head.

I looked back at John Paul, "Dig in, we've got to go." The coffee was still good. The stew was good too. The post-keeper brought out some hats as we ate and we each found one we liked. It was the first time today that I had seen a smile on Paul's face. He had found a derby hat, a city hat, as he called it.

He placed it on his head and said, "Ain't this neat," as he smiled from ear to ear.

"It'll be hot tomorrow we'll need something to keep the sun off us," I explained.

Our business was conducted rather reckless and hasty, but I didn't have much choice. We could not afford to kill any time. I settled on a black hat with a flat brim and trough down the middle of the rim.

"I will get the horse for you," the gentle old man said. He handed me a sack with some food stock in it; he knew without asking that we would need it. Then he was out the door.

John Paul and I had begun to talk a little. He had said to just call him Paul, and I had said that I knew Ms. Melissa would welcome him as a son. I enjoyed the last bit of coffee in my cup, and out the door we went. The Post keeper was there with the horse and a lead rope. I only glanced at the horse, grabbed Banjo, and climbed aboard. Pedro had watered and cared for the horses while we ate.

I tossed him a fifty cent piece and said, "Muchas gratias, Senor."

"Si," he said with a smile.

We were off almost as quick as we came, but felt much better since we had eaten. The two cowpokes had been almost forgotten as we rode off into the night.

❖ ❖ ❖

Two hours later I swapped my saddle to the buckskin we had bought. I felt for the bill of sale in my pocket just in case someone questioned my purchase. I made sure Paul and the black were okay, hitched the lead rope to Banjo and mounted up again.

We had only gone a short distance when the Buckskin jerked her head up and stopped. Then, Banjo and the Black became uneasy.

"Stop!" I commanded firmly, but only loud enough to be heard.

"What is it?" Paul asked as he stopped.

"Be quiet for a minute," I instructed.

We sat motionless for about five minutes and I stepped down. I rubbed the newly acquired horse on the neck and slowly moved out past her. I had only taken two or three steps when I caught the glimpse of something shiny right in front of me.

Return to the Saddle

I sometimes rode with a pair of tight fitting riding gloves on. I had them on now. I reached out and touched the shiny object with my left hand, as to protect my gun hand and keep it close to my pistol. It felt sharp even through the glove.

Once again I got that sickening feeling in the bottom of my stomach. It was a web of glass, metal, and nails tied together with a calf rope. I let my glove hand slide down the web and felt many different objects I thought of poison and pulled one of the jagged pieces close and smelled of it. It smelled absolutely awful.

Confident that they were nowhere around, I struck a match just to look. In all my years I had not ever seen anything like it. It was evil looking. I had never known Indian nor outlaw or anyone to use something like this. Thank God we didn't ride head strong into this thing. It would have been a mad situation. It not only would have cut and spooked the horses, but it was strung up high enough to fall back on us.

"Paul," I called.

"Yes, sir," he answered.

"Get down, let the reins drop to the ground so the horses will be still, and come here slowly. Do exactly as I say."

"Yes, sir," he answered and he got down and started towards me.

I struck another match so he could see me. It had gotten darker, clouds passing through had taken what light we had away. It seemed to match up, medieval witchcraft and a cloudy night.

Paul took one look and asked, "What in heaven's name is that?"

"It didn't come from heaven, I'll assure you of that. Let's get over here to where it's tied off and cut it loose and drag it out of the road. But don't let any of these pieces touch you, they've got poison on them."

When we had finished and I was confident that no one would get into that junk we walked back to the horses.

"Why would someone do that, Mr. John?" Paul inquired.

"It's what you call evil men conspiring with the devil to do bad things, Paul, do not ever allow yourself to get caught up in that stuff son, it has a way of rising up and biting you in the seat of the pants."

"It makes me shiver all over just to think about it," he said.

I started to mount the Buckskin. The horses had had a chance to rest while we worked to clear out a path. Then the thought struck me. I pulled out another match and struck it. There it was laying as big as life. I couldn't believe I had allowed these varmits to get this close to me, twice. The Circle-G brand stuck out like a sore thumb in the light of the match.

Paul walked over and looked, "What is it?" he asked.

"Those two back at the trading post, they were the bad guys we are after. Just think, I had the drop on them and let 'em get away."

Return to the Saddle

"Well, you didn't know," he offered.

"Yeah, and there's nothing we can do about that now, so let's mount up and go."

This time it really got quiet as we rode. We made good time in spite of the darkness. Dawn broke behind us as I swapped back to the App. The Black was holding up good under the light weight of the boy. We ate some food from the sack the old man had given us, watered the horses, and climbed aboard again.

The exhaustion was really settling in, but we had to keep going or else there might not be any reason to go home.

It wasn't long until we had reached our small home. There was no sign of anything. The buckboard was gone, no one in sight. Then it hit me. This was Sunday.

"Paul, this is where you'll be living, take a look around, but don't go far, we've got to keep going."

"Yes, sir," he answered, his politeness was excellent. Then he took off running.

I unsaddled Banjo and turned him loose in the corral. He was about done in. I looked around for something else to saddle, but there wasn't anything else close by.

"Well ol' girl," I said to the Buckskin, "You got anything left?" I rubbed the dust off her back with my gloved hand and quickly saddled up. Paul came running up about the time I had finished. The Black still looked good. Boy that Ben could really pick a good horse.

"As soon as the horses drink a little water, let's mount up, we've got work to do."

"Where is everybody?" Paul asked, "This is a great place you have here, but I ain't found nobody."

"They're at church and that's where we are going," I answered.

"We ain't washed up!" he exclaimed, his old Southern English obvious.

"We don't have much time, let's go!"

We mounted and rode. The Buckskin was still holding up. I'd hate to kill her, but I'd hate worse for somebody to get killed while I ran down a fresh horse.

It took about fifteen minutes to make it to the church in town. I had picked out our little place because it was close to town, to work, to church, and other things we needed.

We tied the horses to the hitching post and I could hear them singing 'Sweet Hour of Prayer'. It sounded so good. We made our way to the front door. I was hoping that everyone was here. That would make it easier to protect them.

We stepped through the front door, and past the racks of hats and coats. There was one or two guns hanging out front. We might need them. This time I kept mine on. They would soon know why.

I pulled the door to the auditorium open and just stood there looking, trying to pick everyone out. Melissa was playing the piano and they were now singing 'Just As I Am'. Her long, pretty hair

Return to the Saddle

was shining in the light. She refused to put it up like all of the other ladies did. I loved it long and hanging down, and her desire was to please me above everyone else.

I couldn't see the Green's. I saw Rich's wife and daughter and my heart sank when I thought about how I would tell her that her husband was dead. Everyone seemed to be here except the Green family.

My gaze turned back to Melissa then to my kids on the front row, then back to Melissa. They were so beautiful. From where Melissa was sitting she could look straight across the top of the piano and see the Pastor and to her left and see the door, and she did.

First, there was a smile, then she saw the gun and the hat still on my head. The smile quickly turned to a frown. She stopped playing and stood up immediately, knowing something was wrong. Everyone turned to look. The Pastor saw me for the first time. I realized that I still had my hat on and pulled it off. Paul did the same, as he stood at my side.

Melissa almost ran to where I was. She wanted to hug me, but she knew something was wrong.

"What's wrong?" she asked, with a worried look.

"Where are the Greens?" I asked.

"They went to get their daughter," someone from the crowd answered.

"How long ago?" I asked.

"About ten minutes," he answered.

"Where did they go?" I asked.

"I believe it was out where Bessie's doll was found," he responded.

"Melissa," I looked at her with urgency, "Keep John Paul with you. I have to get there right away."

I didn't wait to get an explanation or give one. I just crammed my hat back on my head and out the door I went. I knew that Paul would tell all he knew.

I jumped on the Buckskin and whirled around and took off. I sure hoped it wasn't too late.

"Come on girl. Give me just ten more minutes, then you can rest," I begged as I lightly slapped her on the neck. I paced the mare as best as I could. I didn't want her to go down on me before we got there. She held up good.

My mind raced, as the horse galloped, at all that had happened. I thought of the rope I strung up on them, and then they tried to string one up on me, only worse. The horse they rode to chase me with, I was now riding to chase them. This has been quite a turn of events.

Shortly I saw the spot and the Greens climbing out of the wagon. I started waving and shouting trying to get their attention. Closer and closer I came. Then, they saw me and began to smile and waved back at me. They were totally unaware that there was anything wrong.

I came to a screeching halt and shouted, "Get Mrs. Green back in the wagon and get out of here now, this is a trap."

Return to the Saddle

Suddenly a shot rang out and my hat flew off. I jumped from the saddle and jarred the ground hard. It was then that I felt excessively tired, almost as though I wanted to just give up and die.

Another shot rang out and the Buckskin ran off, my rifle still in the boot of the saddle. I scrambled to get behind the rock. I looked and Mrs. Green was down and out in the open. She had been hit.

I grabbed my six-gun and fired three shots up the hill to the same place as before, then ran for Mrs. Green. I grabbed her by the arms and pulled her to her husband's side, behind a rock. He was obviously in shock, never having faced anything like this before. More shots rang out as we fell behind the rock.

A quick check showed me that the bullet had only grazed the top of her head. She would be fine.

"Take care of your wife," I instructed the schoolteacher, "I'll try to hold these two off."

"What do I do?" he asked.

I pulled off my neckerchief and said, "Take this and apply pressure to the cut, she will be fine, just don't let go."

This was exactly the same as when we found the doll, only this time I didn't have Ben or my rifle. This time those two owlhoots up there were determined to kill as many as they could before they got knocked off.

I slid three new bullets in my old Colt. This was my standby pistol. My old reliable was somewhere at the bottom of the Truckee River. This was a good pistol, but I would rather have something I was used to in a bad situation like this.

I moved just enough to get a vantage point to look around. They had us pinned down, no doubt about it. Before, Ben had laid down a valley of fire that allowed me to move, but this time I was on my own with just this six-gun. It didn't look too hot. One of them could keep us pinned down while the other one moved in. Then, I thought of my other gun.

I slid back over by the Greens and pulled out my derringer. "Mr. Green do you know how to use one of these?"

"No--I don't," he answered, his face white as a sheet.

"Well, just pull the hammer back, point where you want to shoot, and pull the trigger. It fires twice, so you only have two chances. They'll be coming after us in a minute so hold the bandanna with one hand, and the derringer in the other. They will have to come in here facing you to get to you. Don't worry, if I have to leave just stay where you are."

There had to be a way out, I just had to see it. I slipped back to my vantage point and stuck my head up far enough to see. Then, a bullet tore at the rock in front of me. I ducked back and moved over a couple of feet and came back up firing. I shot high to cover the distance and elevation, and I saw dust fly and heads drop out of sight.

Suddenly I heard a Winchester bark. What was this? The fellas on top were armed with Henrys',

Return to the Saddle

I could tell by the sound. It sounded like it was coming from over by the road, where Ben was at before. It couldn't be Ben. Anyway Ben had a modified Henry that had a distinctive sound all its own. I risked a peek to see. It was Melissa! Long purple dress and all. Paul was there with her. She must have left the kids with someone at church.

I looked up the hill at the bad guys. I could only see one, and he was looking in Melissa's direction. I took off running, the same way I went before. That one hundred yard uphill dash seemed a lot farther than before. At least I had some cover after that first open spot. I stopped near the end, replaced my empty shells, and looked around. No need to wait. I jumped around the corner and caught one of them by surprise just like the time before. He threw down on me with his rifle, and I blasted him twice from one knee, and down he went. Then, I jumped up and ran over to see where the other one was.

"Melissa!" I shouted, "He's gone after Melissa!" I took off running only to meet my wife after a few steps. She had that rifle pointed right at me, but pulled away when she saw it was me.

"Where's the other one?" I asked frantically.

"I don't know," she answered.

Then the sharp crack of a Henry. We ran to the ledge where the bad guys had been, and looked down to where the Greens were. Standing out in the open was the other bad guy pointing his rifle toward where the schoolteacher and his wife were, behind the rock. How did he get passed me?

151

I heard my derringer pop and saw the man stumble backwards, only to re-aim again. I fired with my six-gun, but it was too far away. Then, beside me I heard that Winchester fire and I saw the man go down, not to rise again. She immediately jacked another bullet in the chamber and aimed again, just in case, but he didn't move.

We stood looking, then Mr. Green came out and looked until he saw us, then waved. I breathed a sigh of relief, and turned and grabbed Melissa and gave her a big hug.

"Oh, Honey, I've never been so glad to see you," I admitted. It felt good to have her in my arms again.

"You too, Honey," she replied.

We walked down to the Greens, by this time the church Pastor and a few others had made their way out to where we were. Paul found us, our kids found us, and boy was it great to be home.

❖ ❖ ❖

Monday afternoon saw my little freight office wrapped up as Ben and the rest rolled in with Bessie sitting up front on the wagon. There were smiles and tears of joy as Bessie fell into her mother's arms. The bandaged wounds didn't seem to bother her.

"Mama, I missed you so much," Bessie cried.

"Baby, I prayed for you to come home everyday," Mrs. Green said, holding her daughter tightly.

Made in the USA
San Bernardino, CA
18 January 2018